Fable Killer

JANE BLYTHE

Acknowledgments

I'd like to thank everyone who played a part in bringing this story to life. Particularly my mom who is always there to share her thoughts and opinions with me. My wonderful cover designer Amy who did an amazing job with this stunning cover. My fabulous editor Lisa for all the hard work she puts into polishing my work. My awesome team, Sophie, Robyn, and Clayr, without your help I'd never be able to run my street team. And my fantastic street team members who help share my books with every share, comment, and like!

And of course a big thank you to all of you, my readers! Without you I wouldn't be living my dreams of sharing the stories in my head with the world!

CHAPTER One

July 6th
10:32 A.M.

Voices.

She heard voices.

He shouldn't be here.

Not yet.

It couldn't be time again already, could it?

And who was he talking to?

That scared her even more.

Her body wanted to fight or run and seek safety that didn't exist, but there was no place to go, and she was too weak to fight.

She prayed unconsciousness came and took her away before the mind-bending pain assaulted her again.

For once her prayers were answered and she slipped back into the comforting darkness.

~

10:33 A.M.

"I'm not sure we should be doing this," Detective Matthew Greer told his partner.

"You saw what I saw," Rylla Franklin returned.

That was true, he had. Didn't mean he thought they should be here. "We don't have probable cause to have broken in here," he reminded Rylla.

"Someone is in here. When we rang the buzzer at the gate you saw her in the window, she called for help."

That's what it had looked like. But really, how could they be sure? They hadn't been able to hear her, but there *had* been a face in one of the upstairs windows, and it *had* looked like she was banging on the glass and calling for them to help her. They hadn't been able to hear her though. Was the house soundproofed?

They had been here by chance. There had been a hit-and-run in the street in the early hours of the morning. They suspected the driver was a man they had been looking for for weeks now in connection to a double murder, so they had been here interviewing residents in the street, wanting to ascertain if anyone had seen anything helpful.

It was the fourth house they went to where they'd seen the woman in the window.

It looked like she was begging for help, so they entered the property and then broke down the front door to get inside.

They had cleared the downstairs and were now standing at the top of the stairs. Taking the first door on the left, Matthew eased it open, and immediately his gaze went to the bed.

A woman lay there, facedown and naked.

She wasn't moving.

Quickly, they checked to make sure the rest of the room was empty, then he went to her. He took in the shackle around her ankle and the chain that ran from it to a metal ring in the floor. Her back was covered in large, bright red welts.

Someone had taken a whip to her.

Sliding his fingers beneath her jaw to her neck, he felt for a pulse. Found one.

"Is she alive?" Rylla asked.

"Yes. Just. We need paramedics."

"She wasn't the woman in the window. There's someone else here."

Rylla was right. Just what had they stumbled upon in this house?

"You stay with her, and I'll check the rest of the house," his partner said.

Alone with the woman, Matthew shrugged out of his shirt, then very carefully rolled the woman onto her back and wrapped her in it. While too thin and too pale, her face was beautiful, and for a moment he stared at it, transfixed.

Long, thick dark lashes fluttered on her cheeks, then her eyes opened slowly. Dazed and confused, when she felt his hand on her shoulder she whimpered and made a feeble attempt to swing a fist at him.

"Shh, it's all right. My name is Matthew. I'm a police officer, you're safe now," he crooned in her ear.

She stilled instantly at his words, her large blue eyes seeking him out and then fixing on him as though she were afraid he may be an apparition, and if she blinked he would disappear.

The haunted gleam in those eyes punched him in the gut, and he wondered the extent of what this woman had endured. Matthew fought to keep a warm, encouraging smile in place and asked, "Can you tell me your name?"

"Grace," came the soft reply. "Grace Bennett."

The name sounded familiar, and almost immediately he placed it, but before he could confirm her identity, her eyelids quivered and closed as she passed out again.

"I found another woman in the room down the hall," Rylla announced, reentering the room.

"What's her condition?" he asked as he reached for a blanket and tucked it around Grace. Despite the warmth of the room her skin was cold to the touch.

"Physically uninjured."

"Well, she isn't. We need to get her out of here."

"I already called an ambulance and reported what we found here."

"She woke up briefly. She said her name was Grace Bennett. I think she's the sister of Detective Bennett." Matthew didn't really know the man very well, but they had mutual friends.

Rylla's green eyes grew wide. "Grace Bennett has been missing for five and a half years."

"Yeah, she has." As he looked down at the unconscious woman, he felt a strong rush of pride and amazement flush through him. If this woman had survived over five years of treatment like this, she had to be the strongest person on the planet.

"There are bolt cutters in the car, I'll go grab them," Rylla said.

Once more alone with the woman, Matthew gently eased her into his lap and surveyed the room. It was large and the floor was covered in a thick and opulent carpet that no doubt felt wonderfully soft to bare feet. The walls had been wallpapered in maroon and gold stripes, the furniture was chestnut and had been polished till it shone. Besides the enormous canopy bed, whose curtains matched the wallpaper and had been tied back around the bedposts with gold tasseled cord, there was a wardrobe and bureau on one side of the room, and a loveseat, a chaise lounge, and two wingback chairs grouped around an open fireplace on the other. There were also two bookcases stuffed to the brim with books, two bedside tables, and a coffee table. Through an open door he spied an exquisite bathroom, every bit as opulent as the bedroom. It was a beautiful prison, but a prison nonetheless, and he wondered if Grace had been kept in here the entire five years she had been gone.

"Here." Rylla returned and handed him the bolt cutters. "EMTs are ten minutes out, if we can't cut the chain, we'll have to ..."

"I'll get it cut," he replied instantly. He didn't want Grace to spend a single second more in this room. The thought of her having to endure her prison any longer made him feel ill. He managed to break the padlock in a couple of tries, then looked from Grace to the door. He wanted to get her out of here, but there was another woman locked up in this house who had no doubt endured the same things she had, and she too deserved to be free of her prison. Torn, he was going to ask Rylla to stay with Grace and go and do the right thing when footsteps sounded on the stairs.

"Rylla? Matthew?"

"In here," Rylla called back, then said to him, "you take her out of here, we'll get the other one."

Scooping Grace's limp body into his arms, Matthew cradled her gently. The bloody blisters on her back looked painful, and he tried not to press against them. He took the stairs two at a time, consumed with the need to get Grace out. Taking her straight to his car, he settled into the back seat with her on his lap. Her cheek pressed against his bare chest, her head tucked under his chin, her hands rested against his stomach, the combination of the three stirred something deep inside him.

A need to protect that he hadn't felt since he was a young boy.

Ignoring it, he wrapped one arm around her and with his other pulled his phone from his pocket and dialed the precinct. Once he had obtained Detective Elijah Bennett's phone number, he called and waited. He couldn't imagine the mess of emotions that would swirl inside the other man when he learned his sister had been found. Matthew couldn't comprehend living for five and a half years not knowing where someone you loved was, but knowing they were more than likely suffering horrendously.

"Detective Bennett."

The voice on the other end of his phone ripped him from his thoughts. "This is Detective Greer. I need to ask you some questions about your sister." He was almost positive the woman in his arms was the detective's sister, but he also wanted to be careful that he didn't give out false hope.

Detective Bennett inhaled a sharp breath, then asked, "What about her?"

"Does she have any identifying marks?"

With what Matthew knew must be an enormous amount of restraint, Detective Bennett replied, "She has a birthmark shaped like a star near her left shoulder."

He had seen it earlier, in the bedroom, but still he slid the blanket and his shirt off her shoulder and traced a fingertip over the birthmark.

"Did you find her body?" Detective Bennett asked tightly.

"No, we found her alive."

"Alive?" he echoed.

"She's alive," he confirmed.

"But hurt because otherwise she could identify herself," Bennett astutely observed.

"She's unconscious, but she woke briefly and told me her name. Before I could confirm who she was, she passed out, so I needed to verify her identity."

"She's really alive?" The man sounded both shocked and guarded like he couldn't yet allow himself to believe the sister he had spent five years preparing to learn was dead, was not.

"Yes, I'm holding her in my arms right now while we wait for the medics. Once I know what hospital they're taking her to I'll call and let you know."

Elijah muttered what sounded like a curse. "We were away for the Fourth of July, I'm a couple of hours away, and my wife, brother, and sister-in-law are maybe a day away." There was a long pause before he spoke again. "You've worked with Ali before, right?"

"Yes, I've worked with her a few times."

"Could you stay with Grace until I get there? I don't want her to be alone." The pain and anguish in his voice was evident, and yet he hadn't asked for specifics about what exactly his sister had suffered.

"I won't leave her," Matthew promised. Even if her brother hadn't asked, he wouldn't have felt comfortable leaving Grace alone given what she had been through.

Voice finally breaking, Elijah asked, "Can you hold your phone to her ear? I know she's unconscious, but I need to talk to her. I need her to hear my voice, I need her to know we're coming."

"Of course." Matthew lowered his phone and held it to Grace's ear. She didn't respond to her brother's voice, and he felt a shaft of concern. Just how badly hurt was she? He had to believe that she would be okay. She was strong enough to survive five and a half years with a monster. Surely, that made her strong enough to survive anything.

Before he even realized what he was doing, he pressed his lips to the top of her head and kissed her blonde head. At the touch of his lips, she whimpered quietly and snuggled closer against him.

~

11:46 A.M.

The alarm had been buzzing for over an hour, yet he had made no move to turn it off.

He was paralyzed.

In shock.

He couldn't believe this was happening.

Someone was in his house.

In his house.

That meant someone had found the girls.

And *that* meant that someone had taken the girls.

His girls.

They belonged to him, and some random stranger had no right to take them.

He was angry. So angry. But greater than the anger was fear. Who was in his house? Emergency plumbers if there had been a burst pipe perhaps. The fire department maybe. But his house was equipped with a sprinkler system that should put out any fires.

That really only left one option.

The cops.

He had a horrible sinking feeling in the pit of his stomach that said it was indeed the police who had breached his house and set off his alarm.

That was his worst nightmare. If the police had stumbled upon his houseguests, then it was all over. They would take his girls away.

What would become of them? They needed him.

What would become of him without them? He needed them.

They would go back to their families he presumed, but would they miss him? One of them had only been with him for a few days, but the other had been with him a very long time, and he had to believe that life without him would be difficult for her. Impossible even.

It would certainly be difficult for him. He couldn't imagine life without them. What would he do with himself? Tending to his girls was the highlight of his day. It was his whole reason for living. It was the center of everything he did. If he could spend every day at home with them he would, but he couldn't. He had to go to work, he had to earn a living so that he could support his family.

And that was how he thought of them, as his family. He loved them, they were everything to him, they were all he had. There was so much he still needed to teach them, so many lessons they had to learn.

But now it was all over.

His home had been compromised, and he couldn't go back, so he had to decide what he was going to do. Where did he go from here? In this moment he thanked his mother, the obsessive planner, that he had pre-prepared a number of scenarios in case he was ever placed in this position.

He didn't have to go back to his house, he wanted to, with every fiber of his being he wanted to, but there was nothing there other than his girls that he couldn't live without. He had access to bank accounts, a car, and another house to live in. He was prepared, had a plan, and ,was confident the police wouldn't be able to identify him, so why didn't he feel happier, more content?

Because the one thing he wanted he had lost.

He would gladly give up everything else if he could just have his girls. Live in the middle of nowhere with basically nothing if it meant being able to keep them.

But he couldn't. Somehow, he was going to have to find a way to go on without them.

With a trembling hand, he reached over and picked up his phone. He stared at it for a good five minutes before getting up enough courage to turn off the alarm.

That was the first step taken.

Next, he opened his car door, climbed out, and walked into work.

That was the second step taken.

Perhaps if he just took things one step at a time, he would be able to do this.

∽

12:21 P.M.

. . .

Matthew had been sitting watching her since she had been tucked into a bed and settled in a quiet hospital room. He hadn't left Grace's side as she had been transported in an ambulance and treated in the emergency room. She hadn't woken up again, but the doctors hadn't seemed to be overly concerned about that. She was quite badly dehydrated so there was an IV in the back of her left hand, delivering fluids to her parched body. A couple of the bloody welts on her back were infected, so she was also receiving antibiotics. Her back had been cleaned and bandaged, and now she appeared to be resting peacefully.

As he watched her, he tried to imagine the horror that she had endured. Matthew had looked up the case file from her abduction, so he knew the basics. Taken from her home while cooking dinner one night, there had been blood on the floor, and he assumed the pale pink scar on her right temple was from the blow that had knocked her unconscious.

Did she know how much time had passed? How had she survived? She had obviously been physically hurt. Had she also been sexually abused? He found it hard to believe she hadn't been, but he wouldn't get any answers until she woke up.

He hoped she woke before her brother arrived. He feared that once her family was around her, she would be less likely to speak about what she had endured, and he needed to know what had happened to her if they were going to find the man who had hurt her.

All of a sudden, Matthew sensed that Grace had woken. She hadn't moved, her eyes hadn't opened, her even rhythmic breathing hadn't changed, but it was like he could feel the change in her.

Standing, he leaned over the bed and made sure to keep his voice calm and soothing. "It's okay, Grace, you're in the hospital."

At his words, her eyes opened slowly as though her lids were very heavy, and lifting them required great effort. Her gaze flitted around the room and then settled on him. He didn't think she would remember him, she'd been conscious for only a few seconds when they had been together, but she whispered his name.

"Yes, you haven't been alone. I've stayed with you." It seemed important that she knew she was no longer on her own. He had expected her to cry, be emotional, or hysterical, but somehow, she managed to remain controlled. No doubt a trick she had learned that had helped her survive. When you were fighting for your life, you didn't always have the luxury of emotion.

"Where are my brothers?" she asked, looking around the room.

"They're coming," he assured her. "On their way now."

She nodded then hesitated, it looked like she wanted to ask him something but wasn't sure how to go about it.

Pulling up the chair he sat beside her, and because he didn't know if she was okay with physical contact, he rested his hand on the bed, right beside hers. "If you have any questions, you can ask me."

"Do you have him? Emmanuel?"

"Is he the man who abducted you?"

"Yes. I'm not sure that's his real name, but it's what he told us to call him. Do you have him in custody?"

"No, I'm sorry we don't. He wasn't at the house when we found you." Matthew hated telling Grace that, and he expected it to be the thing to finally have her break down, but again she surprised him. There was fear in her eyes, but there was also a spark of determination. The right thing would be to let her get some more rest, she certainly needed it, but he had to take advantage of that determination he saw. "Would it be all right if I ask you a few questions? I know you've been through a lot, and it might be hard to answer some of them, but everything you tell me could help us to find him."

Grace nodded her consent.

"Do you know how long you've been gone?"

She hesitated for a moment. "I think it's been five and a half years." Her look said she wanted him to tell her that she hadn't been kept prisoner for so long, but he couldn't.

"It has been." So she didn't dwell on that, he continued on to his next question. "You said the man who took you wanted you to call him Emmanuel. Did you know him? Had you ever seen him before?"

"No. I'd never seen him before."

Emmanuel meant God is with us. Did this man consider himself some sort of God? "What did he look like?"

"Brown hair, he wore it a little long, so it hung in his eyes. His eyes were brown, too, and they crinkled at the edges when he smiled. He was average height, average size, he had freckles," she rattled off.

"How old is he?"

"Our age I guess, late twenties to early thirties."

"Did he keep you anyplace else other than the house where we found you?"

"No. I woke up in that bedroom."

"Can you tell me what happened when you woke up?" Matthew felt his insides clench as he prepared to hear details of her imprisonment.

"I was chained to the bed, and he was there. Emmanuel." Her hands shook a little and she shifted the one beside his a little closer so they just touched. "He told me he was going to fix things, make them better. That he had a lot to teach me and if I was a good girl, I had nothing to worry about." Her hand moved a little more until she hooked her pinkie finger over his, the only indication she wasn't holding it together as well as she wanted him to believe. "He put a metal cuff around my ankle and hooked it to the chain, told me it would allow me to move freely around the bedroom. Then he left. I tried to find a way out, but I couldn't. When he came back, I tried to attack him." When her hand moved this time it covered his completely. "I failed and he punished me. Five days with no food and water, five lashes of his whip each day increasing in increments of five. Five, ten, fifteen, twenty, twenty-five. Emmanuel likes the number five."

Matthew turned his hand so he held hers. "I'm so sorry, Grace. What did he mean by he had lots of lessons to teach you?"

"Fables. He liked fables. They were tests, one girl against another, one lived, one didn't. He brought in a new girl just yesterday, is she okay?"

"She's okay, not injured."

"Good," she murmured, her hand somewhat absently squeezing his.

She looked tired now. Exhausted. Matthew lifted his free hand to cup her head, his fingers absently stroking her hair. "Sleep now, Grace."

"Are you going?" For the first time, a hint of panic tinged her tone.

"No," he promised. "I'm not going anywhere."

That relaxed her and she fidgeted on the bed, presumably trying to get her body into a position that didn't bother her injured back. As soon as she closed her eyes her fatigued body gave out and she drifted off to sleep, leaving him sitting silently by her side, watching over her, protecting her as best he could.

~

2:58 P.M.

Elijah ran through the hospital halls desperate to get to his sister.

He was still in shock.

Part of him believed he would wake up at any second to learn this was just a dream, like the many he'd had since Grace's disappearance. Part of him believed this was some sort of hallucination, that his stressed-out brain had finally snapped. And part of him believed he had imagined the whole thing.

When Matthew Greer had called him and asked about identifying marks on Grace's body, Elijah had felt his stomach plummet. After almost six long years he was about to find out it was over, his sister was dead. Then when Matthew had told him Grace had been found alive, he had immediately felt a swell of denial.

Hope was an interesting thing. It brought with it both joy and pain. Being torn between hoping that Grace was still alive and that one day they would find her was contrasted violently with the hope that she was already dead and no longer suffering.

Five and a half years was a long time.

He and his family had searched for her every chance they had. They worked every lead and spoke to every person who was even vaguely related to what had happened. They had never given up on Grace, but in the end, she had been found on a fluke.

As he rounded the corner of the corridor that Grace's room was located on, he saw Matthew standing outside a door.

His first thought was that Grace was alone.

His second was that he needed to see her. Now. He needed to believe she was really back. Because she was, and he knew that now the hard work would really begin. While this nightmare had been real for Grace, he suspected for the rest of them they had been too focused on finding her to really dwell on what was being done to her, but now it was time to face the nightmare she had suffered head-on. Elijah knew that his baby sister had a long road ahead of her, and part of him wished that his twin brother was here. Jeremiah was a psychiatrist and was much more qualified to help Grace through this than he was.

Intending to barge past Matthew Greer and straight into Grace's room, the younger man blocked his path. It wasn't that Elijah wasn't grateful to Matthew, he was, he could never thank the man enough for finding his sister, but right now he needed to see Grace, and being stopped this close to her was torture.

"Let me past," he snarled.

"In a moment," Matthew remained unfazed. "I just want to make sure you're ready."

"I'm ready," he snapped immediately and reached out to open the door when Matthew stepped aside, then he froze. He hadn't wanted to know any details of what had happened to Grace until he could be here with her. He'd felt like if he had known he wouldn't have been able to make it through the couple of hours it took to get to her. But now there was no more putting off the inevitable. "He hurt her."

"Yes."

"Physically."

"Yes."

"Sexually?" The word almost stuck in his throat.

"She didn't say that he did."

But that didn't mean she hadn't been. "What injuries does she have?"

"She's dehydrated and has some welts on her back."

He winced. He didn't need confirmation that the man who had taken her had used a whip on her. "Thank you. For finding her and for staying with her."

"Of course, she should never have to be alone again."

And she wouldn't. Elijah had no plans of letting Grace out of his sight any time soon.

Ignoring the jitters and doubts that he wouldn't be able to do or say the right thing to help his baby sister, he opened the door and stepped into the room.

It was real.

She was real.

She lay in the bed, her long blonde hair framed her pale face in a wild mess of curls. Although five years had passed since he had last seen her, she looked younger somehow, small and fragile and vulnerable.

He stepped closer to the bed. His hand went to touch her but stopped. Almost afraid to do it. Afraid she was a mirage, afraid he'd hurt her, and afraid that she would wake up and fall apart. Afraid that *he* would fall apart.

Pulling up a chair, he sat beside her bed.

In his mind, he had imagined so many times what it would be like to get Grace back, but none of them entailed sitting in a hospital room beside her unconscious body. He had pictured laughing and hugging which logically made no sense because he knew that when they got Grace back, she would be damaged somehow.

Damaged but not broken. Never broken. His sister was too strong to break.

He sat there for a long time.

Hours maybe.

Just sat and stared at her, transfixed.

Adjusting his position, his chair scraped across the floor, and Grace's eyes flew open at the sound.

Elijah opened his mouth to reassure her, but as her eyes met his he found he couldn't speak.

They just stared at each other.

Grace's gaze was unwavering. Her blue eyes exactly as he remembered them, and yet at the same time, they were almost unrecognizable.

She stared so long and so unblinkingly that he began to worry that she had forgotten him. Matthew hadn't mentioned memory loss, and she had been able to give a partial statement, but she was just lying there not speaking.

Although he supposed he was doing the same thing.

This whole day had been surreal, he could only imagine how much more so for Grace.

Before he could force his lost voice to return, Grace slowly lifted a hand to his face, her fingertips tracing his features.

"Elijah. You're really here."

He pressed his hand over hers and squeezed. "I'm really here. *You're* really here."

Grace all but launched herself at him, wrapping her thin arms around his neck and clinging to him with a strength that belied her fragile appearance. "I thought I would never see you again," she whispered.

"We were so scared you were gone forever," he whispered back. Concerned he was hurting her injured back, he loosened his grip and pulled back a little to study her. There was pain in her eyes, physical and emotional, but there was a strength there that he had never seen in her before. Grace was the baby of the family, a little spoiled, she was sweet and somewhat naïve, but that wasn't the woman he saw looking back at him now.

Of course they had never been going to get back the same woman who had disappeared, but still seeing his sister looking not quite like his sister was disconcerting, and he knew they were all going to have to find a new normal.

~

3:34 P.M.

It was an odd feeling leaving the hospital. Matthew felt like he left something behind.

As he got out of his car and went to meet up with his partner so they could do a thorough search of the house where Grace and Barbara Lack had been kept prisoner, he reminded himself that he had to forget about Grace. Well, not forget about her as far as this case went. For as long as it took to find the kidnapper, she would be a part of his life. They'd have to interview her at least one more time, probably more, and then there would be the trial. But that was all, Grace was nothing more to him than a victim in one of his cases.

That was it.

So why did it feel like he was lying to himself?

How was it possible to get attached to the woman in the few hours he'd spent with her?

Especially when he had been turned off relationships after destroying the ones he had with his family. If he couldn't even hold onto the people he was bound to by blood, the people who were supposed to be there for him no matter what, how could he expect to make any other relationship last?

Matthew already knew the answer to that question.

It was because Grace was different. There was a strength about her that seemed near impossible. Did he think she would be able to hold it together indefinitely? Of course not. Sooner or later the woman would be in for one major breakdown, she was only human, it was inevitable, but he admired the fact that she had answered his questions without complaint, to the best of her ability, and all before she'd even had a chance to be reunited with her family after such a long time being held captive.

Grace Bennett was something else and he was going to have to find a way to get rid of that tingly feeling he got in his stomach every time he thought of her. She'd just been rescued after years of being held prisoner by a maniac, even if she really hadn't been sexually assaulted the last thing on her mind was dating.

Let it go.

"You're back."

He startled a little at Rylla's voice and hoped it didn't show. The last thing he needed was anyone catching on to this weird little crush he seemed to be developing. "Yeah, Elijah Bennett showed up at the hospital."

"How's Grace doing?"

Matthew tried to surreptitiously search Rylla's green eyes to see if she had any indication that he was allowing himself to get attached to Grace in an oh so inappropriate way, but he couldn't see anything. "Better than I would have thought. She told me that the man who held her captive wanted to be called Emmanuel, and that he didn't sexually assault her, but he had a fascination with fables. He used them to test the girls, apparently, they were lessons. Grace said one of them would live and one die."

"Did she know this Emmanuel?"

"No. Said she'd never seen him before."

"Did she give a description?"

"She did but it was nothing remarkable. Still, when she's stronger we'll have a sketch artist work with her, see if we can get something useable. Who's the owner of the house?" It would be much easier if they could just get the name off the deed and go and arrest their perpetrator. This weird connection he felt to Grace wasn't like him at all, but wanting to bring closure to a victim, that was. He'd been there, knew what it was like to feel like you had been left hanging, like you weren't important enough to warrant anyone's time or effort, and he tried to make sure no victim ever felt that way. He *would* find Emmanuel, nothing else was an option.

"House is owned by an eighty-two-year-old woman named Mable White."

"So not our guy. We need to find out what we can about Mable, hopefully she has a grandson named Emmanuel." While he would love that to be the easy answer, there was just as much possibility that the kidnapper had simply killed the old woman and taken over her house. That's what he would do if he planned to abduct girls and keep them locked away. No one would have cause to look for you in a house that didn't belong to you.

"From what I've seen so far, this house is more like a hotel than a home," Rylla said as they both walked through the front door. "There are no personal papers that I've been able to find. No photos on the walls, just a few pieces of generic art. Furniture is all beautiful quality, I presume it was all Mable's, but it looks like he removed whatever personal touches used to be here. There are no knickknacks, no throw pillows, no anything personal."

Matthew let his gaze roam the living room. The house wasn't large, downstairs there was a lounge room, a kitchen and dining room, and a den with a large open fireplace. Upstairs there were three ensuite bedrooms, one for the kidnapper and two for his victims, of who he knew there had been many. "If he was related to Mable, you'd think he would have kept a few of her personal items as mementos."

"I agree," Rylla said. "What were these tests Grace told you about?"

"I don't know, I didn't get time to ask her too many questions, she was still weak and exhausted. Tomorrow we'll have to go back to do a more thorough interview." Not something he looked forward to even though he knew it had to be done. Making Grace relive every single detail of what had happened to her was going to upset her, maybe even cause the breakdown he knew would be coming, but he didn't have a choice. The kidnapper was still out there and that meant they had to do whatever it took to stop him or more women would be hurt.

"I was just wondering where he did them." Rylla spun in a slow circle, taking in the entry foyer, and the three open doors leading to the downstairs rooms. "The yard is a nice size, and while someone would have a hard time seeing over the big stone fence, he still couldn't take his victims outside. We're in the middle of the suburbs, all they would have to do is call for help."

If the kidnapper had gone to the effort of soundproofing the house, no way would he be careless enough to allow his victims access to anyone. The furniture in the downstairs rooms, and the bedrooms, meant there wasn't a lot of available space, so depending on what these fable tests required he wouldn't be able to do them in any of the rooms.

"Basement?"

"I haven't been down there yet, but there was a door in the laundry room that I assumed led down to one," Rylla replied.

"Let's check it out." Tomorrow when they interviewed Grace they'd get more answers, but he seemed to be consumed with the need to try to remove any of her burdens that he could, and the more he knew the less they'd have to quiz her on.

He and Rylla walked through the kitchen door and into the tiny laundry room. There was another door in there and they opened it. Flipping on the light switch at the top of the stairs, they headed down into a small, open space. Across one wall there were boxes stacked. Written on the sides he could see the words Christmas decorations printed neatly, and he felt anger surge. Had the man really taunted his victims by decorating for Christmas or were these just leftovers from Mable White?

Since Emmanuel had gotten rid of all the rest of the woman's things except the furniture, it stood to reason that in fact he *had* decorated for

Christmas. Grace told him that her kidnapper had wanted to teach her lessons, was it possible the man was delusional and didn't just derive some sort of sick pleasure from killing the woman, but actually believed that he was helping them?

If that was the case, then it meant there was a possibility he was going to come back.

If Grace was more than just a random woman he'd plucked off the streets—and the fact that he had kept her alive for so long meant there was a good chance she was—then it definitely made sense that the killer might try to come back for her.

Protecting people was who he was, it was what he did, only when he'd tried to protect his family it hadn't worked out the way he'd thought it would. In fact, it had ended up costing him the very people he had been trying to save.

He *would* save Grace, do whatever it took to make sure she was free to live the rest of her life on her own terms, and it had nothing to do with a shadowy thought in the back of his mind that if he saved her, she might want him.

CHAPTER
Two

July 7th
2:41 A.M.

Kick your legs.
    Don't stop.
    Go slow.
    Not a race.
    The water splashed around her, and Grace had to work to still her racing heart. He wanted her to panic and that was the only reason she didn't. No way was she going to give Emmanuel the satisfaction of knowing just how much he and his stupid fable games terrified her.
    On principle, she would rather die than allow him to glimpse the absolute horror she felt every single day. The only thing that had kept her alive so long was the very fact that she had managed to cling to a control she hadn't even known she possessed and fight through every single one of his tests.
    So ... kick your legs.
    Don't stop.

Go slow.

Not a race.

The mantra had saved her before and it would save her again, but there was nothing she could do to save the woman floundering helplessly in the other pool.

It killed a tiny piece of her each time another one of the girls died, but she was powerless to do anything to stop it from happening. That was Emmanuel's game, or his lessons as he thought of it.

One lived, one died, and there was no way she could allow herself to be the one who died. Certainly not now when she had fought for so many years to keep herself alive. She had a family at home, one who would be going crazy searching for her, and because they would never give up on her, she couldn't give up on them.

Grace hadn't ever known she was this strong. As the baby of her family, she had been spoiled, she was used to getting her own way. She hadn't really been into the whole camping, shooting, hunting, outdoorsy kind of things the rest of her family liked, but they all made an effort to do things she liked too. She'd never once felt left out or like she didn't belong, she'd been sheltered a little, definitely coddled, and looking back she knew she had been very naïve.

That naivete was long since gone.

She was tougher now, stronger, and yet as she watched the woman beside her go under and struggle to get her head back above the surface, she had to fight the urge to panic. Determination stopped her from letting her movements grow frantic and jerky, Grace kept them slow and steady. Emmanuel would leave them in here until one of them drowned and panicking wasted energy.

Slow and steady wins the race.

How many times had she heard that since he brought her here?

Of course, she'd heard of fables growing up, but she had never met anyone who was obsessed with them before she'd met Emmanuel.

The woman went under again, this time she could barely get her head back up. It had been hours since Emmanuel threw them into the pools, exhaustion weighed at her limbs, but still she fought against her instincts to scramble as fast as she could.

Next time the woman went under she didn't come back up, her move-

ments were slower now, barely movement at all, and Grace knew that she had won.

As the woman jerked once or twice, then went still, her wide empty eyes staring sightlessly in death, she knew it was a hollow victory.

She had won this time, and she would *win next time, but this woman was dead. How many more would she have to kill to win ...*

Grace woke with a start, unsure where she was. Her heart thundered in her chest like it was trying to race its way right out of her body so there would be no more death.

How much more could she take before she just turned dead inside?

"Gracie?"

She turned her head and saw two figures standing beside her bed.

The room was dimly lit, but her moment of panic very quickly faded away as she recognized them.

"Jeremiah," she squealed happily and pushed herself off the bed to hug her other brother. There was a tug of pain in the wounds on her back, but she didn't care, anything was worth it for a chance to hold onto someone she loved.

"Hey, sweet little girl," Jeremiah said as he sat on the edge of the bed beside her and hugged her back. There was moisture on her cheeks, but it hadn't come from her own eyes, she hadn't cried since that very first day she'd woken up in Emmanuel's house. After that it had been all about survival, but now that she was back home, she didn't know how to live any other way. For five years her entire existence had been about staying alive and doing whatever she had to not to die. How could she ever learn to live her life normally?

"You okay, Gracie?" Elijah asked.

Forcing herself, she relaxed. She'd learned to live with survival as her only goal, so surely it couldn't be all that hard to learn to live normally. It was really only doing in reverse what she'd done before. She could do that.

She *had* to do that if she wanted to live.

Survival was still the name of the game only now it was a different kind of survival. What would have been the point of everything she had done over the last five years if now that she was free and had the chance to live again, she wasted it?

No. She couldn't waste it, she would learn to be normal.

"I'm okay," she replied and pulled back enough that she could swat at Jem's shoulder. "But don't call me little girl, I haven't been a little girl in a really long time."

Pain flitted through both her brothers' eyes, and she knew they were thinking about the innocence that had been stolen from her by Emmanuel, but that wasn't what she had meant. She'd just meant that in her mind she'd stopped being a little girl around the time she was eight, and she was now almost twenty-eight years old.

Time.

Looked like it would take time for her family to adjust to their new normal just like it would for her. They had been living this nightmare right along with her. As much as she knew she'd had the worst of it, at least she had known where she was and what was happening to her. They hadn't known anything except that she was gone, and they couldn't find her. No doubt their imaginations had come up with some pretty horrible scenarios.

She offered them both an encouraging smile. They'd been strong for her many times in the past, if she had to be strong for them now, she could do that. Thankfully, her stomach chose that moment to growl loudly, breaking the tension, and making them all chuckle.

"I know it's early, but any chance of some breakfast?" she asked, settling back down against the pillows. It hurt her back to lie against the small wounds, but she'd certainly endured worse pain, and being here, safe, and free, with the big brothers she'd hero-worshipped for as long as she could remember, the pain drifted into the background.

"First thing Laynie did when we got back was make your favorite cinnamon rolls," Jeremiah told her. She could tell he tried to get a read on her. Unlike Elijah and his wife, Allina, and Jem's wife, Allayna— Laynie and Ali were also twins. just like Jem and Elijah, and their parents had been best friends and grown up together—he hadn't joined the police department. Instead, he'd become a criminal psychologist, and right now he was trying to shrink her. Too bad for him she had perfected the art of hiding her emotions over the last five years.

"Laynie and Ali are here?" she asked. Since they weren't in the room, she'd just assumed that her brothers' wives were at home. If she'd known they were at the hospital she would have demanded to see them already. They might not be blood related, but they were every bit as much her siblings as her older brothers.

"In the waiting room. We didn't want to overwhelm you by coming in all at once," Jem told her.

"I'm anxiously waiting to be overwhelmed," she joked. Family was what had kept her going, it was what made her fight every day. That drive to survive had made her do horrible things, things she would forever regret, but it had all been done for this. To finally be back with the people she loved.

"I'll go get them," Elijah told her.

Grace ignored Jem's prying gaze. If he was trying to get a read on her she wasn't going to let him. She had a new goal now, well two of them, the first was to help the cops find Emmanuel and make him pay for what he'd done, and the other was learn to be normal again. There was one thing she had learned while she was Emmanuel's prisoner, and that was that you had to fake it till you made it. If she didn't feel normal, then she had to pretend that she was and sooner or later it would become less act and more real.

When her two sisters-in-law came bursting into the room, running to the bed, crying, and hugging her, Grace realized she wasn't completely faking it. Her heart did melt a little as the people she loved crowded around her, cocooning her in a little bubble of warmth, safety, and love.

They weren't the first ones to make her feel safe since she had been rescued a few hours ago.

The first person to do that was Detective Matthew Greer, and she had no idea what to make of that.

~

9:00 A.M.

"Okay, let's get started," Captain Heidi Kramer announced. His boss sat at the head of the conference room table, but like always, she wasn't

sitting still, in one hand she spun a pen, and in the other she rhythmically squeezed a duck shaped stress ball. The woman was in her fifties,
tall, thin, bony face, always looked stern, like an elementary school prin-
cipal, but she was a good boss, fair, listened, made sure that her team was
taken care of, and was always supportive of them. "Matthew, Rylla, you
guys want to start?"

Matthew glanced at his partner who nodded at him, then turned to
face the room. Besides his boss, his partner and himself, Grace's sister-in-
law Allina's partner Jonathon Dawson was also present—no doubt to
represent the family—and one of Matthew's favorite crime scene techs
Kane Curtis.

Unable to resist, this morning before coming to the precinct, he'd
stopped by the hospital to check on Grace. She'd been asleep, her body
needing the rest to recoup years' worth of living on a never-ending
adrenalin ride. But according to her brother Jeremiah, she'd woken
during the night and spent some time catching up with her family
before falling asleep again.

It was clear from the psychologist's voice that he was worried about
how his little sister was handling everything. Matthew totally got that,
for now Grace seemed to be doing fine, according to her family she
hadn't shed a tear yet and had been acting like nothing had happened.
They all knew that couldn't possibly be true, no one could be okay after
living through what Grace had, literally no one. But he supposed as far
as their job went having a calm and in control victim worked to their
advantage.

Heidi cleared her throat and Matthew realized he hadn't said
anything yet. Grace was proving to be a distraction, one he couldn't
really afford. He'd dreamed about her last night, only she'd been naked,
and in his bed, begging him to make love to her. It was completely inappropriate, and never going to happen, but he couldn't seem to stop
thinking about her.

Something he was going to have to get a handle on.

"Rylla and I searched the house yesterday, but we couldn't find
anything to give us any indication on who Emmanuel really is. We did a
little canvassing of the neighbors, and best we could figure out from a
couple of them who had been in the area for a while, is that Mable

White hasn't been spotted in around seven years. While they have seen a guy going in and out of her house, no one really knew much about him. He introduced himself as Emmanuel, but we're assuming that's not his real name. They all said the same thing; he isn't the kind of neighbor you have over for dinner. He said he was Mable's grandson who had moved in to help her because she had developed dementia, but Mable White was widowed just two years after she was married, had no children, and never remarried."

"Chances are he looked for a vulnerable victim, settled on Mable White, killed her and just moved in," Rylla added. "It makes things easier for him. He doesn't tell anyone she's dead, he keeps her name on the house and all the utilities, he gets access to her bank accounts, keeps collecting her social security which means everything is paid for, and if the house is found he's virtually untraceable."

"We need proof that Mable White is dead," Heidi said. "We need CSU to go over the property. If he killed her and didn't want anyone to know it, then chances are she's buried somewhere there."

He and Rylla had come to the same conclusion because it was the most logical answer. "When I spoke with Grace yesterday, she told me that Emmanuel wanted to teach her lessons, that there were tests, apparently they were somehow linked to fables."

"Fables?" Jonathon echoed. "I can see the media dubbing him the Fable Killer if that gets out."

Matthew could too. He hated it when the media decided to give a name to a killer, it made them out to be some sort of almost fictional being. That was when people let their guards down, didn't see a threat, and started to see the killer as a character in a play rather than a real person, a real threat, and someone who hurt real people.

"Kane, did you get any forensics we can use?" Heidi asked, turning her attention to the crime scene tech.

"We have his fingerprints and DNA, we're running them through every system we have but so far no hits," Kane replied. "If we get anything I'll get you guys know immediately, but there's always the chance we won't."

That was the thing with forensics, often times they were more helpful in proving your suspect was the one you were looking for, rather than finding you a suspect. While he would love it if the fingerprints or DNA gave them the name of Grace's abductor, he wasn't going to count on it.

"What we need," Heidi said, "is a full statement from Grace Bennett."

Jonathon stiffened. While the man had never met Grace, he'd been partners with her sister-in-law Allina for a couple of years now and had bonded with her and her family. Everyone in the precinct had spent time trying to help the Bennett family track down Grace, but Matthew was sure that Jonathon had put in more hours than the rest of them.

"I don't think Grace's family is going to let you near her, not yet," Jonathon said.

"Allina, Elijah, and Allayna are all cops, and Jeremiah is a criminal psychologist. I'm sure they all know the importance of getting the victim's statement," Heidi said, the determination in her gaze said Grace would be interviewed, and today.

"What about the other victim?" Jonathon asked.

"We've talked to Barbara Lack," Rylla replied, "but she was only taken a few days ago and doesn't know much. She hasn't participated in any tests, although Emmanuel told her he had lessons he wanted to teach her. Grace has spent years with this man. She's the one who is going to give us the best information."

None of them were unsympathetic to Grace or her family, they all knew how hard things were for all of them. Just as they also knew how important it was to talk to Grace.

She was the key to unraveling this whether they liked it or not.

"I know what you're all going through," Rylla said softly, for a moment her green eyes lost their spark. It was only six months ago that Rylla had lost her sister and then herself been kidnapped and almost killed. Matthew had been there that day, along with Rylla's now husband Nate. He didn't think he would ever forget the fear he'd felt ravaging his body when they weren't sure if they'd find her alive. Although she covered it well, he knew Rylla still struggled with what had happened to her, and in an effort to forget had thrown herself into work and raising her thirteen-year-old niece Emmy, and recently turned ten-year-old nephew Mac.

"We all get it," he assured Jonathon. "And just like it was hard for you to watch Clara give her statements, her sisters too when they were hurt, you knew it was the right thing to do. The only thing we can do. The Bennetts know that too. We're all on the same side here. All we want is for the man who hurt Grace to be held accountable. Unfortunately, the only way to achieve that is to talk to Grace."

Even though he said the words—and believed them one hundred percent—there was a queasy feeling in his stomach as he thought of asking Grace more questions, having to watch her answer them with a determination he wasn't sure any of them could understand. Grace had already proven herself to be strong and a fighter, the best way for her to begin recovering from her ordeal was for everyone around her to recognize that strength.

Matthew knew from experience how much it hurt to fight for your life, and those of the people you cared about, to do whatever it took to stay alive, only to be shunned for it later. While he knew Grace's family would never shun her, they needed to support her, however it turned out she needed that support.

Grace had done her part, she'd been strong, she'd fought hard, now it was time for someone to be there to hold her hand while she worked through it all. Was it completely wrong of him to want to be there to do just that?

His preoccupation with the woman wasn't fading, if anything it kept growing.

He was in for heartbreak if he let himself get attached which was exactly why he never did let himself get attached. Grace was faced with the daunting task of rebuilding her life. She'd lived through a hell he could never understand, the last thing on her mind was men and relationships.

Yet he couldn't stop feeling something for her no matter how much he tried.

Or how much he wanted to.

～

11:52 A.M.

. . .

"I know you're just trying to protect her, but have you asked her what she wants to do?"

The voice was familiar, and Grace immediately placed it as belonging to Matthew. She got a little thrill hearing it which was definitely odd because she was pretty sure she had more than enough to be worrying about right now without developing some sort of crush on one of the detectives working her case.

Maybe it was the promise of distraction that it gave.

If she thought about Matthew, she didn't have to think about Emmanuel.

Curious as to what was going on out there, instead of heading from the bathroom to the bed, she headed for the hospital room door.

"Asked me what I want to do about what?" she asked. Matthew stood in the hall along with Elijah and Jem, who were standing in front of her room like guard dogs.

Elbowing past her brothers she looked up at Matthew. He was taller than her five-foot-three frame by close to a foot, so she had to crane her head back to meet his gaze. He was better looking than she remembered from yesterday. She'd been too out of it then to appreciate his chiseled jaw, his warm brown eyes, there was a spark of something in there that touched her inside and she couldn't not smile at him.

"Good morning, Matthew."

"How are you feeling today?"

Grace shrugged. "Pretty good, I guess. Still tired, and a few of my wounds were infected, but I'm feeling better than yesterday. What's in the bag?" she asked, eyeing the bag with the logo for her favorite burger joint on it.

"Chicken burger and fries, I heard that's your favorite." Matthew's smile was warm and genuine as he held the bag out to her. In his eyes there was none of the pain she kept seeing when she looked at her family. There was respect there, admiration, but she didn't kid herself that he wasn't aching with pain for her, it was just that she seemed to be able to feel it even though she couldn't see it.

Odd.

"You brought me lunch?" Her eyes lit up and she reached for the bag, opening it and inhaling. A sigh escaped, it smelled delicious. Emmanuel had fed her well enough, but it was always his choice of meals. It had been so long since she'd had any control over even the simplest things in her life, and even though Matthew had chosen this food he'd picked it because it was her favorite. That was sweet.

"You think you can bribe her with lunch?" Elijah asked. He had his arms crossed over his chest and scowled, he looked so ridiculous she rolled her eyes and smacked his shoulder.

"It's not a bribe, he's a cop, I'm sure he has to ask me questions. I'm happy to talk to you," she told Matthew. Maybe happy was a bit of an exaggeration. She wasn't *happy* to talk about what she'd lived through, but she was more than prepared to do it so that Emmanuel was caught. The last thing she wanted was for him to stay free and be able to hurt more women like he'd hurt her. So, she would do whatever it took to help the cops find him even if it was hard, and her brothers weren't going to get in the way.

"Gracie," Jem started in that overly patient psychiatrist tone that had always irked her.

"No, don't *Gracie* me. I've had enough of my power taken away from me and I won't ever allow anyone to tell me what to do ever again. From here on out, I am making all my own choices. So, Matthew, I'll answer your questions."

With that, she turned and walked back into her room. There was a chair over by the window and she pulled the tray table over to it and sat, pulling out her food. It smelled so good, and her mouth was watering by the time she lifted the burger and took a bite. A bit of the sauce dribbled down onto her chin, but she didn't even care, this tasted so good, and it was amazing to eat the food she liked again.

"Do we need to give you a bib?" Matthew teased as he sat on the bed.

Grace laughed, and it felt so good that she almost cried.

Almost.

Seemed like she'd somehow lost that ability somewhere along the way.

"It's so good," she mumbled through a second mouthful of burger. This was quite possibly the best meal she'd ever had. "Thank you."

"You're welcome. I'm glad you like it."

"Love it," she corrected. "You can ask your questions if you don't mind me eating while I answer." Even though she would do this, she wasn't looking forward to it and wanted it done and over with.

"This is my partner, Rylla Franklin," he said, indicating a woman with red curls and pretty green eyes.

"Hey, it's Oakland now," Rylla said, lightly punching his shoulder.

"Oops." Matthew looked only marginally apologetic, and from the twinkle in his eyes she knew he was teasing his partner. From the smile on Rylla's face, she knew it and didn't mind because they both knew they were trying to put her at ease. "Rylla only got married two months ago. Sometimes I forget she changed her name."

"Congratulations," she said to Rylla. Before she'd been abducted, she had been excited about falling in love, getting married, and having her own family, but now ... now she couldn't think that far into the future without getting overwhelmed.

So she didn't.

Instead, she took a fry and ate that. "Hey, I don't think so," she said when Matthew reached out and snagged one.

He laughed and ate it anyway, but then he sobered, and she knew he was ready to get down to business. "I know this isn't easy for you and I wish there was another way ..."

"But there isn't," she reminded him. "I'm the only way you're going to find him, I know that. So go, ask your questions."

"We're going to have a sketch artist come by later to work with you on a sketch of Emmanuel. Is that okay?" Matthew asked.

"Of course."

"You told me yesterday that Emmanuel had tests for you and the others."

"Fables," she said. She didn't get the connection, but it seemed to make sense to Emmanuel.

"Where did these tests take place?"

"The basement. There's a room down there, the door is hidden in the wall."

"Can you tell me about these tests?" Matthew asked gently.

For a moment she munched on her fries, needing a few more seconds to get herself together. She wasn't proud of the things she'd done, but she also knew she'd do it again if she had to. Survival meant doing whatever it took to live.

Whatever it took.

"Grace, if it's ..."

"No, it's okay," she told Rylla. Then she focused her attention on Matthew because he provided her with the stability that she needed to be able to do this. "The games were based on fables, at least they were in his mind. His favorite one was the tortoise and the hare, but he also liked the ant and the grasshopper, the gnat and the bull, the lion and the mouse."

"How did he turn the fables into lessons, tests?" Matthew asked.

Her mind wandered to her nightmare. The water test he'd done several times, but it was just one of many. "The tortoise and the hare he would throw us both into a pool of water. They were separate pools or large plastic boxes, maybe ten feet tall. He'd throw us in, then fill it up. You had to swim or drown. The trick was not to panic because if you panicked and went too fast then you'd tire out. Slow and steady wins the race," she murmured, how many times had she heard him say that.

"Were all the tests like that?" Matthew asked. His appearance didn't change but again she felt rather than saw his anger. He was furious about what she'd been put through, and while she appreciated it, it didn't change it.

"Yes. Variations of things like that. Ropes, knives, nooses, all sorts of horrible things." Grace hesitated, she didn't want to tell them, but if it was important and she didn't, and Emmanuel hurt more people because of it she would never forgive herself. Straightening her spine, she set her food down and met Matthew's gaze squarely. "I ..." This was harder than she thought it would be. "I ..." she tried again. "I ..."

Matthew stood and came to crouch beside her chair. He took her hands and held them in his, his thumbs brushing across her knuckles. "Grace, if he made you do something to those women it wasn't your fault. Whatever you did you did to survive. It is not your fault.

Emmanuel is the one responsible, he's the one to blame, not you. Okay?"

When he said it, she almost believed him.

"Did he make you hurt them, Grace?" Rylla asked, her voice just as gentle as Matthew's had been.

She nodded. "Sometimes. Not always, it depended on the lesson."

"I'm so sorry that happened," Matthew said, and he sounded so sincere that she couldn't not believe him.

"Yeah, me too." There was a dullness to her voice that even she could hear, but she shoved it away. This was too important to mess up because of her feelings. She could deal with them later. Maybe. But right now, the cops needed her, and she wasn't going to let them down. She owed it to the women whose lives she had played a part in ending to make sure Emmanuel paid for what he had done.

"Do you know the names of the other victims?" Matthew asked.

"No, I'm sorry. He never told me their names. We were both kept locked in our rooms, I never had a chance to talk to them. But I remember their faces, I'd know them if I saw them again," she said fiercely. There was no way she would ever forget those faces. It was the only way she had been able to do her part in keeping them alive somehow.

"Hey, Grace." Matthew's thumb hooked under her chin and tilted her face so she had no choice but to meet his gaze. There was no judgment there only a kind of understanding that told her somehow, he did actually understand. "You did good."

A weight eased slightly off her and she found her smile was genuine. He could never know how much those words meant to her. "Thank you."

CHAPTER

Three

July 8th
12:03 A.M.

Nervous energy buzzed through him.

That was wrong.

He was never nervous.

Well, at least not anymore.

Emmanuel had been doing this a long time now, seven years. Before that, he'd dreamed about it. For as long as he could remember, he'd had a fascination with fables, with learning lessons, growing, and attaining a higher level of consciousness.

It seemed only fitting that he help others.

When he'd first started, he never expected that the same woman would keep learning his lessons, keep beating his tests, and doing whatever it took to survive. Grace Bennett's innate ability to survive intrigued him. In her, he saw a version of himself. He saw the little boy who was so desperate to make things better, to take away his parents' pain, to understand why his sister had done what she'd done, and make it through each day and get stronger.

Grace was the very definition of a survivor.

Now she was gone.

Anger took away his nerves. It wasn't fair. Why did they have to take her away from him?

Didn't they know he needed her?

She needed him too. Emmanuel was positive that their survival had become a codependent thing. He couldn't exist without her, and she couldn't exist without him. How could she? After what had happened to her, she'd needed someone to help her understand and process things. He had done that for her, he had taught her so much, helped her reach the same level of consciousness that he had. But now that she was gone, what would happen to her?

Would she regress?

Take her own life?

Hurt someone else?

Would she try to see him? Try to find her way back to him?

The thought that she might be trying to get to him and someone prevented her nearly choked him. He had been there for her, he had helped her, he had made her all but invincible. She had to be needing that back.

Or maybe she had finally outgrown him?

Emmanuel had always believed that the Universe had a way of making things right. Sometimes it didn't feel like it, especially when things weren't going the way you wanted, but in the end, it knew what it was doing.

It was why he had tried so hard to understand the Universe. It was the one thing that made him feel unsettled. There was power in knowledge, power in understanding what was happening to you, and power in knowing the way the Universe worked.

Fables.

It was why he loved them so much. They were the key to understanding the Universe and he had dedicated most of his life to studying them, learning them, and memorizing them all by heart. He had done his best to impart that same knowledge to others, and even though it didn't always work he had done his best, and that was all you could do.

He couldn't stop.

There were others out there like him. Those who had been hurt, who had been abandoned, who had been left to try to figure out the world all on their own. They needed him and he couldn't just leave them to flounder alone.

So here he was.

Emmanuel eased open the back door. Picking locks was something that came naturally to him, he wasn't sure he'd ever struggled with it, and it certainly came in handy. It wasn't like he could just knock at their front doors and be let in. They didn't understand yet that he was only trying to help them.

But they would.

At the end, they would realize what he had done for them, and they would die grateful, a little closer to understanding the Universe than they would have been without him.

As he crept inside the quite house and closed the door behind him, he wished he'd had someone like himself to guide him when he was just a boy. After his sister's death, his parents had all but forgotten about him. He'd been only nine, and growing up virtually by himself had been terrifying. There had been no one to explain things to him, to support him, hold his hand, encourage him, or cheer him up. It had all been left up to him.

How different could his life have been if he'd had a mentor?

If he hadn't been alone?

These women didn't realize how lucky they were.

This house was small, just the one large room downstairs. He wasn't a fan of these open plan houses. Emmanuel liked small rooms, they felt cozy and safe, he felt protected and tucked away, it was almost like a cocoon.

Taking quiet, confident steps, he headed for the stairs and made his way up them. He'd been in her house earlier, while she was still at work, so he knew there were two bedrooms upstairs, and that the one on the left was hers.

The bedroom light had turned off an hour ago, but he'd waited in his car a full sixty minutes just to make sure he had given her plenty of time to fall asleep. The last thing he wanted was to have to fight her to get her out of here. He would do it because it was the only way he could help her, but he didn't enjoy hurting women.

At the top of the stairs, he found the door to the spare bedroom open but the door to Patrice's bedroom was closed. Carefully, he turned the handle and pushed the door just far enough open that he could fit through.

Then he froze.

The bed was empty.

Emmanuel spun in a circle and as his back turned to the bedroom door something slammed into him from behind.

He grunted and went down hard on his hands and knees.

"I won't be hurt again," a voice hissed. Patrice's voice. The woman mustn't have been asleep, must have heard him coming and hidden, waiting for the perfect time to strike.

She hit him with something in the back of the head and the world shimmered around him.

What was happening?

Why was the Universe doing this?

Patrice was a nice woman, she'd been hurt, he knew that, but she wasn't violent. In fact, she was a librarian at the local library, she worked several children's programs there. On the weekends, she volunteered at a nearby animal shelter. Everything she was was about helping others, protecting them, caring for them. That was why he'd known that she was one of the ones he was sent to help.

So why was she fighting him like this?

"I'll kill you before I let you put one of your filthy hands on me."

"I'm not here to hurt you," he said.

"Yeah, right," she scoffed. "That's why you were breaking into my home at midnight."

Emmanuel turned just as he saw something glint in the moonlight streaming through the open window.

A knife.

He lunged up off the floor, grabbing Patrice's wrist as he did so. She screamed and thrashed in his hold, but he didn't stop.

Using her own momentum against her, he kept the knife hand moving down only instead of allowing the blade to slice through his flesh he plunged it into Patrice's own.

"Oh," she said, dazed as she staggered backward when he released her, the handle of the knife protruding from her belly. She made a gurgly sound as she hit the wall and slid down it until her backside hit the floor.

"Why did you make me do that?" he asked. Tears streamed down his cheeks. This wasn't what he wanted. He had come here to help her, he wanted to save her, teach her, and help her understand. Why hadn't she got that?

"P-please," she murmured, blood bubbled out of her mouth, and she reached out for him.

He should go, she'd screamed, she might have alerted a neighbor, and had probably called the cops once she realized he was inside her house. It was definitely the safer option to get out while he still had a chance.

But he found he couldn't leave her.

She was dying and he didn't want her to die alone like his sister had.

So, he knelt beside her and took her hand. Her fingers clenched around his, but he didn't know if it was because she needed his comfort or if it was just reflex. Her face was contorted in pain, and she looked so sad, so scared.

The merciful thing to do would be to put her out of her misery.

Emmanuel reached out and took hold of the knife, twisting it.

Patrice screamed in pain and tried to push his hands away, but he held on and twisted the knife again.

Why wouldn't she hurry up and die already?

He didn't want to see her like this, it pained him. He'd come here to help her, to save her, if only she had understood that. It didn't have to end this way.

Keeping one hand on the knife handle as he twisted it a third time, his other hand lifted to palm her cheek. "It didn't have to be this way," he whispered. "I didn't want it to be this way. It's okay, let go, don't prolong things. Let your pain go, don't fight, Patrice."

Her eyes widened at the use of her name, but then they clouded over, and he could tell she had almost passed.

Emmanuel gave one more twist of the knife, and Patrice made a choking sound before she went limp, her eyes rolling back in her head.

"It didn't have to be this way," he said again. He stood and carefully scooped her into his arms, carrying her over to the bed and laying her down. Emmanuel ran his hand over her hair once and then he left.

This would never have happened with Grace.

She wouldn't have fought him.

She would have understood.

He had to get her back.

~

8:13 A.M.

She was bored.

Which was stupid given that she had spent the last several years stuck in the same room all day every day. At least on the good days, on the bad days she was taken down to the basement and forced to fight for her life.

But this morning Grace felt stronger, better. The wounds in her back were healing, the infection mostly gone, and she'd gotten enough sleep that her body was finally starting to recover from over five years of never sleeping properly. Her body had been used to living on an adrenalin high, she never slept properly, jumping at every small sound. Now that she was safe, she could finally shut down enough to actually rest and her body had taken advantage.

Today though she felt good, and she wanted out of this hospital room.

Grace didn't really know what was going to happen to her. Her house was long since gone along with most of her possessions. Before she'd been taken, she had been finishing off college, prepared to follow in Jeremiah's footsteps and become a criminal psychologist.

Now she couldn't see herself doing that.

No home, no job, no anything.

"Morning."

She had been seconds away from falling apart as she realized that she might be alive, but her future was still every bit as uncertain as it had been when she was trapped in Emmanuel's house, but at the sound of the voice she brightened. Boredom averted, melt down averted, thank goodness for Matthew Greer.

Despite her earlier melancholy, her smile was genuine when she turned from the window to see him standing at her hospital door. "How did you get past the guard dogs?" she asked. Her brothers and their wives were great, but they were being so protective of her that it was almost stifling. It wasn't fair to be annoyed with them about it because she knew how much they had hurt and suffered when she was taken, how hard they had fought to find her, how scared they were to lose her again, but she needed freedom.

"Told them I had a question for you. I lied," he said with a wink.

"Then why did you come?" she asked, curious. Matthew had been great with her yesterday, sensitive when he asked his questions, but also not pulling any punches. He hadn't sugar-coated things, and had treated her like she was strong and capable, not a helpless, fragile little victim. Not that she thought any victim who fell apart was doing anything wrong, in fact they were probably a whole lot healthier than she was playing things right now. But Emmanuel was out there, and she had to be strong, had to help the cops, so holding it together was a must.

"Breakfast." He held up another bag, this one from a nearby diner that made some of the best pancakes around.

"Pancake Pete's? They don't do takeaway," she said, but still crossed the room to take the bag.

"Talked them into it just this once."

"Charmed them into it is more like it." She opened the bag and inhaled the scent. Never before had she thought too much about the fragrance of food, it was always just there, but smelling the food, enjoying it, it was all part of the experience, one that had been denied her in Emmanuel's house. Then she'd eaten not because she enjoyed it but because her body needed fuel. From now on, Grace wasn't going to allow herself to take the small things for granted because it was the small things that made life ... life, rather than just an existence.

"You think I'm charming?" Matthew waggled his eyebrows making her laugh. He was good at that, making her laugh.

"You know you are. I bet you turn on the charm anytime you want to get your way."

"Guilty as charged."

The grin he shot her was even more charming and she felt that same little tingle in her chest. "You bought a lot of pancakes. Do you think I'm going to be able to eat all of these by myself?"

He shuffled a little and she wondered what had made Mr. Charming all of a sudden nervous. "I thought I might have breakfast with you before I go to work."

Her mouth dropped open. That was the last thing she expected him to say. "Really?"

"Unless you have plans," he teased.

She laughed again. "You know I don't. My grand plans at the moment consist of hanging out in my hospital room, and if I'm really lucky, taking a walk to the cafeteria."

"Then how about breakfast outside?"

Now her eyes lit up. She would love to go outside. In the five and a half years since she had been kidnapped, she hadn't once stepped outside. Sometimes Emmanuel allowed her to walk around the house, but all the windows were bolted shut, the doors locks, everything soundproofed and isolated. It was like being locked in another Universe, so close to the real world and yet so far removed.

As much as she would love to go outside, feel the fresh air and sunshine on her skin, she wondered what Matthew got out of it. She had definitely gotten a whole lot more cynical over the last few years.

"Why do you want to have breakfast with me? Do you have more questions?" Maybe the food was just a bribe. If it was it was completely unnecessary, she was prepared to do anything the cops asked her if it would help them find Emmanuel.

He looked surprised by her question, but there was no guilt in his eyes. There was *something* there though, and she realized he wasn't surprised at her question, he was surprised by his own desire to spend time with her.

Grace warmed a little more inside.

"No, I don't have any questions, I just thought it would be ... nice."

She tried to hide her smile a little. Grace didn't think he would appreciate her being able to read him so easily. For some reason, she suspected that Matthew kept a lot of himself locked down tight, only allowing people to see the projection he wanted them to. What was he hiding beneath the charming exterior?

"I would love to have breakfast outside, and I guess you can join me," she teased.

This time he rolled his eyes at her. "Come on," he said, grabbing the bag and indicating a wheelchair he'd brought with him.

She curled her nose up at it. "I don't need that."

"Hospital orders. Come on, I'll push it really fast."

That made her chuckle. "I'm not five you know."

"Oh, I know." The heat that warmed her this time had everything to do with her lady parts. As shocking as it was to her, her body was actually responding to Matthew's. How was that even possible? Yeah, she'd had boyfriends, and her body always responded to them, but after everything she had been through she hadn't thought it was possible for her to feel anything for a man. She hadn't lied when she'd told him Emmanuel hadn't touched her sexually, he hadn't, but ... there was what had happened before her abduction.

A little dazed, Grace dropped down into the wheelchair and waved at her brothers as Matthew pushed her past them. They waved back, but didn't look pleased she was going somewhere with Matthew, still they didn't interfere and she appreciated that. Maybe they were finally catching on to how important it was to her to make all her own decisions.

Her confusion over what she felt whenever she was around Matthew dissipated when he pushed her outside and she was hit with a barrage of feelings and sounds. Car engines, birds chirping, people talking, someone somewhere was drilling, and she heard the toot of a train. The sun was warm on her skin, and there was a gentle breeze that caressed her and ruffled through her curls.

They were in a small courtyard where there was grass, flowers, and trees.

She needed to touch them, smell them.

Pushing up out of the chair, she kicked off the slipper boots her brothers had brought for her to wear, left them where they fell, and walked over to the grass. When her bare feet touched the soft blades she curled her toes into them, trying to absorb the sensations as though they could be stolen away from her again.

Unfortunately, Grace knew that they could be.

All of this could be snatched away in a second. She could be right back in that room, no fresh air, no freedom, no anything.

She walked across the grassy area to the tree and ran her fingertips along the bark. It was rough beneath her touch, but she enjoyed it, it was so real, so alive. She reached for a leaf next, the different texture brought with it an excitement like she was a baby experiencing the world for the first time, and in a way she was.

Grace felt like she was being reborn. The old Grace was gone forever, she was a different person now. That didn't have to be a completely bad thing. This new Grace could take the best parts of both who she had been before and who she had learned to be and become a better version of herself.

There were flowers planted around the base of the tree, and she sunk to her knees in the grass and leaned over to press her nose into the sweet-smelling gardenias. The white petals were soft and beautiful, and she made up her mind now that as soon as she got her own place again, she was going to plant flowers everywhere, ones that bloomed all year round so she would never be without beauty in her world.

A butterfly fluttered past, all bright blues and purples, and she watched it in wonder as it flittered through the air and landed on the flower closest to her. Buzzing captured her attention, and she watched as a fuzzy little yellow bee collected pollen from first one flower and then another.

How had she managed to survive so long without access to nature?

Grace would watch from her window, see people go about their lives, watch the sun climb across the sky, the rain drum down, but she'd felt so detached from everything to do with the real world. Now she was back, and it just felt so wonderful she was almost surprised she didn't sprout wings and go flying through the sky herself.

Scrambling to her feet, she turned to find Matthew watching her, a smile on his face. She didn't think, just acted, jumped at him, and kissed his cheek. "Thank you so much."

His arms came around her and he hugged her gently, for a moment she thought he had breathed in her scent much like she just had with the flowers, but she was sure she had to be wrong. He might be being nice to her, might enjoy making her smile, but there was no way a man like him could want anything with a woman like her.

And did she even want him to?

Being attracted to him was one thing, but wanting more was foolishness. She was in no position right now to be starting anything with anyone.

Still, she held onto him extra tight for a moment longer than necessary.

～

1:37 P.M.

"Why did you want to come back here?" Matthew asked, unable to completely hide a shudder as they walked back into the basement's hidden room at Mable White's house. Yesterday afternoon her body had been discovered buried in a shallow grave in her own backyard. Preliminary autopsy indicated the woman had been strangled, and Matthew felt a whole new level of rage to this Emmanuel for what he had done to the elderly woman, Grace, and all the other victims.

"I don't know exactly," Rylla said, walking around the room.

Matthew watched his partner, if he didn't, he was going to focus too much on the torture chamber, and images of Grace, trapped in here and fighting for her life, would smother him. He had no idea how the woman had managed to survive, how she managed to wake up every day and keep fighting. Giving up would have been the easier option, a way out of the hell Emmanuel had trapped her in, but she hadn't done that.

It would have been so easy for Grace to just stop living. Even now that she was free it would be so easy for her to give in and let the darkness consume her. Nobody would blame her for falling apart, for being depressed, terrified, and unable to function.

But that wasn't Grace.

Nope, his curly girl held it together like a champ.

He wasn't kidding himself. Matthew knew that Grace was likely depressed and terrified, possibly on the way to suffering post-traumatic stress disorder and would definitely fall apart at some point. But he also knew that she was strong. Stronger than he could ever hope to be. She had a wonderful support system of extended family there for her, she had a psychiatrist for a brother, cops for family. She had people who would fight alongside her.

She had him.

Matthew didn't know what had led him to the hospital this morning, he just knew he wanted to see Grace. Wanted to try to take her mind off everything, even if just for a moment. The pancakes seemed like a good idea, after all, who didn't like pancakes, and since he knew she'd been trapped inside for so many years taking her outdoors seemed natural. Her brothers wanted to wrap her up in cotton wool and lock her away, he knew it was because they wanted to protect her and he couldn't fault them for it, but he knew it wasn't what she needed.

What she needed was to find her wings again.

Watching her touch the trees, and smell the flowers, stare in wonder at a butterfly, laugh as the breeze tousled her hair, tip her face back to absorb the sunshine, he knew he was right. She needed to be free, needed to remember what it was like to live, she needed people to believe in her so when the dark days came for her, she could fight through them just as she'd fought through everything else.

And he'd be there by her side as she did it.

He was getting way too attached. Sure, they had the connection of her family and him having mutual friends, but there was no reason why he should be taking any special interest in her. He certainly didn't feel anything for the other woman found in Emmanuel's house. Barbara Lack was just another victim to him. He felt the same drive to close her case, and give her closure that he always felt, but that was it.

Nothing like what he felt with Grace.

This wasn't him. He didn't let people get close. Ask anyone who knew him, and they'd say he was a charming, laid-back guy. He worked, went to the gym, played basketball, he was the guy you called if you wanted to hang out, have some fun, but weren't in the mood to go drinking. He didn't drink because knew what happened when people lost control of their faculties. No one knew about his past, no one got close, he dated until the woman started developing genuine feelings then cut her loose. He liked his freedom, liked not being tied down, liked not having to risk getting hurt.

Grace made him want to throw all that away.

It made no sense, he didn't understand why he felt this way. It was probably the safer option to cut off contact, allow Rylla to lead any interviews they needed, and lay off the visits to the hospital.

It was the right thing to do.

He just didn't think he could do it.

"Matthew?"

"Sorry," he said, forcing himself to focus. What Grace needed most was to know her tormentor was no longer out there. "What did you say?"

"What do you think of this?" Rylla pointed to a wooden contraption that he couldn't even begin to figure out what its purpose was. Grace hadn't gone through all the tests she had been forced to do to stay alive, they hadn't thought it was necessary. If at some point they needed to know everything he'd made her do, they would get her to detail them all. Not something he looked forward to.

"I don't know what it's supposed to be," he said.

"Me either, but that's not what I meant. I mean this is nothing, not something you can buy in a store. It does what he wanted it to do."

Matthew nodded as he caught on. "He had to have made it himself."

"Right." Rylla walked further across the room and stopped beside the large plastic box that Grace had told them about. "And this. I mean we know what he used it for, but it's not something you can buy. Again, he must have made it."

"Some of these things anyone could make." He gestured to the large hole dug in the floor, it was filled with what looked like quicksand. "He could dig that, get quicksand—although not sure where you get it from, that's something we should look into—but he has to have some sort of carpentry skills."

"Maybe building in general." Rylla had walked over to the far wall and ran her hand along it. "This basement is large, bigger than the house. We can check other houses in the street but I'm guessing its bigger than theirs. That doesn't necessarily mean anything of course. There could be plenty of reasons why someone wanted a huge basement when they built this house, but what if that's not the reason."

"What if he built this himself." It would make sense, there was the hidden door that led to this part of the basement, just like Grace had told them, and someone had to have put that in. Somehow, he couldn't see Mable White needing a hidden room down here so there was a good chance it was Emmanuel. This space was large. It probably went close to the property lines. If he'd extended it himself then it would be a big job, hinting that he didn't just have carpentry skills but building knowledge. "Good thinking, Ry. We should take the sketch of Emmanuel and start hitting up some of the local builders, see if anyone knows him."

"Hopefully, we can get a name for him, I'd bet anything it's not Emmanuel."

"Agreed." Matthew took a look around the room as he and Rylla headed for the door, this place gave him the creeps. Every time he looked around it all he could see was Grace fighting for her life. "I hate being in here. I can't imagine how horrible it was for Grace and his other victims."

Rylla shuddered and rubbed her hands over her arms even though it was warm and stuffy down here. "I can."

Even though she didn't talk about it much, Matthew knew his partner still struggled to deal with nearly dying. Throwing herself into work and helping her nephew and niece heal from the loss of their mother could only do so much. If you didn't deal with trauma, it festered and grew into other problems. He didn't want that to happen with Rylla or Grace.

"Hey, I'm here if you need to talk," he said, resting a hand on Rylla's shoulder.

She smiled up at him. "I know you are. You're a good guy, Matt, and Grace is lucky to have you in her corner. Can I give you some advice?"

"Sure."

"Don't push her to talk until she's ready. Everyone is ready to talk in their own time. It's different if we need to ask her questions for the case, but when it comes to personal things just let her come to you when she's ready."

"Personal things?" he asked. He hadn't said anything to imply to anyone that he was after anything more with Grace than wanting to be her friend. Hadn't even allowed himself to think it.

Rylla grinned. "Don't even bother trying to pretend that you aren't developing feelings for her. I've seen the way you look at her. You care about her."

"I'm just trying to be a friend."

"Keep telling yourself that."

As he looked after Rylla as she climbed the steps out of the basement, he realized he couldn't keep pretending. He did care for Grace, but she had been through a horrible trauma, and he knew that men and relationships were the last thing on her mind. What she needed was a friend, not a boyfriend.

Maybe it was time he accepted he wanted more so he could set that aside and do the right thing by Grace. Friendship was all that could be between them. It was what she needed, and it was best for him too.

Friends.

He could do that.

~

3:38 P.M.

Grace shifted uncomfortably in her bed.

She wasn't in pain anymore. Her wounds were healing nicely and most traces of infection nearly gone. She'd slept so much over the last few days that her body was pretty much caught up which meant she was bored.

Again.

This morning she'd had fun outside with Matthew. After she'd thanked him for being so thoughtful, they'd sat in the courtyard and eaten their pancakes before he'd taken her back to her room and gone to work. She knew he would be focusing on her case, but they didn't talk about it. For some reason thinking that all he saw her as was a case depressed her.

Did she want to be more?

There was no denying the fact that she was attracted to him. Even with everything she was dealing with there was a spark there, at least for her. Did he feel it too?

She wasn't going to bring it up, it was way too embarrassing. No doubt he was just being nice by hanging out with her because of who her family were. With both her sisters-in-law and one of her brothers in the local police department, and her other brother a renowned criminal psychologist, she wasn't surprised she was getting special treatment.

Not that she wanted it.

She had taken lives. If anyone deserved special treatment it was the women who had lost their lives at her hand and Emmanuel's hand.

It was easy for Matthew to say that Emmanuel was responsible for the things he had made her do, but it was much harder to believe it when you were the one who had done the killing. Taking innocent lives to save her own, like she was somehow more important than them, it wasn't right.

Grace was ashamed of some of the things she had done in the name of survival.

Some of the games had just been about surviving, like the water game, but some of them hadn't ended the other woman's life. After those games, Emmanuel had handed her a gun and told her to finish them off.

The temptation to turn the gun on him was strong, but she was chained up with the key to the chain upstairs. If she killed Emmanuel, all she was sentencing herself to was a long, slow death from dehydration.

Once again, her own survival had won out.

Tears burned her eyes but didn't fall, and Grace threw back the covers and climbed from the bed, curling her hands into fists, and digging her fingernails into her palms. She needed to hurt, needed to suffer like the other women had suffered. It wasn't fair that she got to be rescued, that her body was healing, her strength returning, that she was able to enjoy the feel of the sunshine on her skin and smell the sweet fragrance of flowers.

She should be dead.

Frustration burned inside her, and she dug her nails deeper into the soft flesh of her palms. It should be her that had died, but since it wasn't she should be suffering. There was a part of her—a small part—that wished she was dead. It seemed the only fair answer, and yet another part, the bigger part, knew that she hadn't wanted to kill those women. She would forever be haunted by their faces and their pleas for mercy, but she wanted to live.

Grace still wanted to live, wanted to be normal, get back the life she had lost or build a new one. She wanted all those things she just knew she didn't deserve them.

Would Matthew still come by to visit her with burgers and pancakes if he knew that she had literally killed innocent women, kidnap victims? He would be repulsed by her.

She was repulsed with herself.

Her nails dug deeper, and she could feel blood dripping from her palms. It felt almost ... good to bleed.

No doubt Jem would love to know that. He'd be all over it, he was itching to figure out some practical way to help her, but she couldn't talk to him as a patient to a therapist. He was her big brother, Jem and Elijah had been fifteen by the time she came along. Her parents' unplanned, later in life, change of life baby. While she hadn't been an unhappy surprise, her parents had been older, her brothers already in college before she started school. They'd been almost like parents to her rather than siblings. There was no way she could sit with Jem and tell him everything Emmanuel had made her do and how she felt about it.

Maybe she could talk to Matthew?

For some reason she felt like he would understand.

Which made absolutely no sense.

Why would Matthew understand anything about what it felt like to take a life?

Even if he'd had to kill someone in the line of duty, it wasn't the same thing at all. If he'd killed any suspects, they'd been criminals, dangerous, he'd had to do it to protect himself and others. What she'd done was take the lives of innocent women who had never done anything to hurt anyone and were just trying to fight to live like she was.

What she'd done was wrong.

Justifiable perhaps, but still wrong.

It would be better if she could just stop thinking about Matthew as anything more than one of the cops working her case. He wouldn't want her if he knew what she'd done, probably didn't want her anyway. Fixating on him was just a way for her to try to cope, it didn't mean anything.

Just because she kept glancing at the door to her room, hoping to hear footsteps, hoping to see his smiling face, hear him laugh, and stare at the twinkle in his warm brown eyes, it didn't mean that she liked him.

Definitely didn't.

Because he was just doing his job. She might go so far as to say they were developing a friendship, but that was it.

Pain sparked in her hands, and she had to force her fingers to uncurl. She'd asked her brothers and sisters-in-law to give her some time alone today. They all knew they couldn't hover at her side indefinitely, if they tried it was going to stifle her healing and moving on, make them all become co-dependent, and sooner or later she would resent it. Not because she didn't love them to pieces, but because she wanted to grow strong again and have her own life, and that was something she couldn't do if she had people constantly hovering over her.

Now, though, she wished they were still here. She felt lonely and unsettled, a sense of foreboding shadowing her. That was just because she'd spent the last five and a half years living on high alert, Grace knew that, but still she wanted the feeling to go. She was home now, free, healing, going home tomorrow, well, to Jem and Laynie's house until she could get a job and her own place. There was no need to keep preparing herself for something awful to happen.

"You're safe now, Grace. Get over it," she told herself aloud.

Turning away from the window, she walked into the small bathroom and turned on the faucet. While she waited for the water to warm, she grabbed some paper towel and scrunched it up, then she held it under the water and began to clean the little crescent wounds on her palms. Her nails had dug deeper than she had realized, and it took a little while to get the bleeding to stop.

Once she had, she dried off her hands and headed back into the bedroom.

Just as she walked through the door something slammed into her, shoving her up against the wall.

Hands were around her neck before she even had a chance to process what was going on, preventing her from screaming for help.

Emmanuel.

He wore wearing black jeans and a black hoodie. He had the hood up and under it he wore a baseball cap pulled low, but she had spent years as his prisoner, she would know him anywhere.

"Don't fight me, Grace," he whispered. His hands around her throat were tight enough to make it hard to breathe, but not tight enough to cut off her air supply. He didn't want her dead, just unable to fight back. "I know it wasn't your fault that they took you away from me, but you know that you need me. I helped you, you know that. If it wasn't for me, you wouldn't be alive. I protected you, taught you, helped you grow strong again. You can't live without me."

As he rambled, Emmanuel dragged her toward the window. Her room was on the second floor, they could jump, but they were both likely to wind up injured in the fall.

It wasn't being hurt that terrified her, she'd been hurt at Emmanuel's hands plenty of times before but knowing she might wind up his prisoner all over again, that left her barely able to function.

She'd never see her family again, never get to rebuild her life, never even get to ask Matthew if he felt that same spark she did.

That wasn't fair.

Anger took hold inside her, and she planted her feet and pulled back against him. If he was going to take her again then he would have to fight for it, no way was she going easily. He should know by now that she would fight for her life with everything she had, and while she would forever be haunted by the women she'd been forced to kill, nothing would make her happier than taking Emmanuel's life.

~

4:00 P.M.

What was he doing?

Yeah, that was probably something he should have figured out before he got here.

Matthew looked at the bouquet of flowers in his hand. He'd gone with something bright and colorful, something fun and whimsical, and he thought the daisies certainly achieved that. Plus, they reminded him of Grace. She was strong and enduring just like them, but also beautiful and sweet, and the image of her yesterday, laughing as she was on her knees in the grass, smelling the flowers was forever a part of him now.

That was the Grace he wanted to help her find.

That Grace was still inside her somewhere. Yes, she'd had to harden herself, toughen up, her very life depended on it. It would take a long time for her to stop living in survival mode, stop expecting the worst, preparing to battle to the death, and by the time she got there she wouldn't be the same person she'd been before Emmanuel took her, but he wanted to help her see that didn't have to be a bad thing.

The new Grace could encompass all the best qualities of who she'd been before and what she had learned about herself as Emmanuel's prisoner.

The most important thing was that she was safe now.

Safe and so very strong.

For so long she had been fighting by herself. There was no one to watch her back, no one to stand guard and give her a rest, no one to hold her while she absorbed the horror she'd been through. It certainly wasn't rational, but Matthew couldn't seem to stop himself from wanting to be that person for her.

So, he was here, and he had determined to be honest and upfront with her, let her know he liked her, wanted to be her friend, an ear to listen when she was ready to talk, and if and when she was ready for something more, if she felt the same way he did, then they could explore something else.

It was pure craziness.

Matthew had been so sure he wasn't interested in dating. He knew how breakable families were, how easily they turned on one another, and while the idea of anything happening between him and Grace terrified him, he couldn't get rid of this feeling in his gut that kept screaming at him not to let her go.

Maybe the fact she was going to need time to heal before jumping into anything was a good thing for both of them. It gave him the time he needed to get used the idea as well.

As he turned into the corridor that Grace's room was on, he realized there was no one hanging around outside her room. She must have somehow managed to convince her brothers and their wives to go home. The Bennetts had been keeping a vigil at the hospital, all but moving in here to be close to Grace. He wondered what she'd said to convince them to leave for a while.

However she'd managed it, he was glad to have a little time alone with her without her overprotective big brothers standing guard. He got why they were protective, but it didn't make things any easier. Matthew had a feeling that if they knew what he'd done he would be the last person they would want taking an interest in their baby sister.

He lifted his hand to knock on the door when he heard a scuffle.

What the ...?

Matthew flung open the door and dropped the bouquet when he saw a man dressed all in black trying to drag Grace to the window.

To her credit, she wasn't going quietly.

The man—who had to be Emmanuel, anything else would be way too big of a coincidence—had his hand around her throat but she was fighting him.

He crossed the small room in three strides, but in that time, Grace rammed her knee up into her assailant's groin then followed up with a palm strike to his nose.

The man granted and released her then looked up and registered Matthew's presence.

He would have bet anything that he was about to wrap this case up right here and now. Emmanuel's obsession with Grace was going to be his downfall. He'd get the guy in cuffs, read him his rights, call back up, make sure Grace was okay, get this guy to the station and interview him then have him locked away for the rest of his life.

That wasn't what happened.

Emmanuel took one look at him, swore, then bolted for the window.

With a last look over his shoulder at Grace, he picked up the chair, slammed it into the window and jumped.

Matthew also swore then bolted to the shattered window. On the concrete beneath Emmanuel staggered to his feet, injured but capable of moving if the way he swayed and limped as he ran off was any indication. Matthew briefly thought of calling out to the people below to stop the man, but Emmanuel was likely to kill anyone who got in his way, and he wouldn't risk innocent bystanders.

Swinging a leg over the ledge he was about to risk the same jump Emmanuel had just taken when small hands curled into his shirt.

"Don't, please. I don't want you to get hurt."

Grace's words stopped him, and he climbed back inside and turned to find her staring up at him. There was uncharacteristic vulnerability in her gaze, and he reached for her and pulled her into his arms. She was trembling and came willingly, wrapping her arms around his waist and pressing her face against his chest. While she didn't shed a tear, she did cling to him, and he felt that all the way down to his soul. She was putting her trust in him, allowing him to hold her, allowing herself to seek comfort from him, and that act of trust cut a huge sliver out of the wall he'd built around his heart to protect himself from more pain.

There was no doubt in his mind that Grace was worth the risk.

When he felt her stop shaking, he gently grasped her shoulders and eased her back just enough that he could see her. The first thing he noticed was the blood staining the front of his white shirt.

"You're hurt," he said, wincing internally when he heard the words come out somewhat accusingly. It wasn't her fault Emmanuel had attacked her and he certainly didn't blame her for it.

She looked from his blood-stained shirt to her hands and shook her head. "It wasn't Emmanuel. I was thinking earlier, and I accidentally dug my nails into my palms a little too deeply. It's nothing. I'd cleaned them up, but they must have started bleeding again when I fought Emmanuel." A spark flickered in her deep blue eyes as she obviously realized that she had just fought for her life and won again, only this time it was against her tormentor.

"Let me see." Circling her wrists, he lifted her hands and beneath the blood smudges he could see four small crescent-shaped cuts on each palm. Reaching for the tissues on the tray table, Matthew carefully blotted away the blood. Grace watched his every move, but when he reached out to palm her cheek her gaze lifted. "Are you okay? Did he hurt you anywhere else?"

"No," she replied softly. "He grabbed me as I came out of the bathroom, put his hand around my throat, and shoved me up against the wall." He still held one of her wrists, but her other hand lifted, her fingertips stroking along the red marks on her neck. Matthew took her hand, stilled it, and entwined their fingers. "He started pulling me toward the window but I wasn't going with him. If he wanted me, he was going to have to fight for me."

He grinned in spite of the fear still lodged in his chest. "That's my girl."

Her eyes widened at his words, but instead of withdrawing a small smile curled up one corner of her mouth. "I'm not going to be a victim ever again."

"You did good, Grace."

She nodded. "He'll be back though."

"Did he say that?"

"He told me not to fight him. He said that he helped me, taught me, saved me, and that I couldn't live without him."

No doubt it was part of Emmanuel's delusion that he believed he was somehow helping the women he abducted with his crazy fable games, but he couldn't help but feel like maybe there was something specific the man believed he had saved these women from. Something he'd have to talk to Grace about later. He also had to call in what had happened, let Rylla know and call Grace's family. Get a doctor in here to check her out, have CSU come and examine the room, make sure

Grace was settled somewhere else tonight, and post a guard on her door.

So many things to do, but instead of doing any of them he reached for Grace again and pulled her into his arms, needing to hold her.

~

7:27 P.M.

"You look like you're thinking really hard over there."

Grace smiled in spite of her gloomy mood when she heard Matthew's voice and felt him come up behind her. He didn't touch her, hadn't touched her since he'd held her in his arms after he'd saved her from Emmanuel. She had fought as hard as she could, even managed to get him to let her go, but Grace wasn't kidding herself, she still knew that if Matthew hadn't shown up when he did that Emmanuel would have gotten her out of the room.

She was sure Matthew was trying to be respectful of her. Although she'd answered a ton of questions there were still things he didn't know about her time with Emmanuel, and she was pretty positive he didn't believe her when she'd told him Emmanuel hadn't sexually assaulted her. As much as she appreciated him trying not to do anything to upset her, the last thing she wanted was to be treated like a china doll.

There was no way she was breaking.

After fighting so hard and for so long, if she fell apart now that she was back home it would be like all that was for nothing. Like all those women had died for nothing.

The only way she could honor their memory was to live her life to the fullest. She would forever carry the burden of their souls, but maybe she could make up for it a little, set those souls free if she lived for them and for herself.

Turning, she took a step toward him, closing the space he'd left, and placed her hands against his chest. It was hard as a rock beneath her stinging palms and she liked that, he felt strong, and sturdy, and safe. "Thank you for saving me today."

Matthew smiled, lifted his hand but hesitated a moment before brushing his knuckles across her cheek. "You were doing a pretty good job of saving yourself."

"It wouldn't have been enough though." She didn't mean it to sound like she was sulking or complaining because she wasn't, merely stating a fact. She would have to do something about that. Whenever her brothers had tried to convince her to let them teach her how to shoot, she'd always said no. Grace hadn't liked guns and violence, had wanted to focus only on the good in life, but now she knew better. Now she wanted to learn how to defend herself.

"You did good, I'm proud of you."

The words could have sounded condescending coming from someone else, but she could see the admiration in his eyes so she knew that he meant them, and they made her feel good. Probably better than it should considering she still didn't really understand this pull she felt toward him or even know if he felt it too.

"Where's your family?"

Matthew had been close by since Emmanuel jumped out the window, but he'd also tried to be respectful of her need to be with the people she loved. He really was a respectful guy, maybe that was why she was getting attached. "They went to grab some dinner."

"I'm surprised they left."

"Yeah, they didn't want to." That was an understatement, they'd fought about it, but in the end they had relented. "Given last time I asked for some time to myself Emmanuel almost kidnapped me again they didn't want to go, but I've made it clear that what I need most right now is autonomy. I need to be able to make my own decisions. So, we compromised, they're having dinner in the cafeteria before coming back to spend the night."

"If you want some time alone I can leave," Matthew offered.

"No." The word burst out with a little more force than she'd intended, but she wanted him to stay. "I mean, if you need to go that's fine, but I'd like you to stay," she said, suddenly shy.

The smile Matthew gave her told her that not only did he want to stay but he loved that she wanted him to. "Did you eat dinner yet?"

"I wasn't hungry earlier, but let me guess you're going to feed me again."

"Pizza should be here any minute."

"Mmm," she moaned in anticipation, her mouth already watering. "You're really ticking all the comfort food boxes."

Matthew's large hand settled in the small of her back. He turned her and guided her to the window where there was a small table and two chairs. This new room was a little larger than the other one, and there would be a police guard on her door tonight as well as her siblings being in the room with her.

"What's your favorite comfort food?" Matthew asked as they both sat.

"My mom's mac and cheese," she answered without hesitation. She had loved that stuff, when she'd been very small she'd gone through a stage where it was all she would eat. "First meal I'm cooking for myself when I get out of here is that."

"Your mom won't make it for you?"

"My mom had a really bad stroke just a few months before I was taken. She's in a nursing home, can't move and can't speak. She's so brave, she's still in there, trapped inside her own body, but she hasn't given up. I'm going to go see her on the way to Jem and Laynie's house tomorrow. I can't wait to hug her." Even though her mom couldn't talk, Elijah and Ali had gone over there the first day she'd been found and they'd called the hospital and she'd talked to her mom on the phone.

"I'm sorry, that's rough. What about your dad?"

"He died not long after I graduated high school. He was only fifty-eight but he had a massive heart attack and was dead before help could arrive."

"I'm sorry," he said again. "That's really rough."

"Yeah, I'm lucky to have my brothers though, and Ali and Laynie. They're all fifteen years older than me so they kind of helped raise me. I love them all so much, and I know I'm lucky to have such a supportive family."

Before she could ask about Matthew's family, there was a knock at the door and a nurse stuck her head in. "Pizza's here."

"Thanks," Matthew said as he stood and took the steaming box.

"One cheese pizza for the lady." He bowed and held it out to her, and she giggled.

"You have certainly been doing your homework, Detective Greer. You knew my favorite burger joint, that pancakes are my favorite breakfast, and that I only eat cheese pizza." She opened the box and took a slice, her eyes closing as the taste consumed her as she took her first bite.

"All part of the service." Matthew took his own slice and the expression on his face as he watched her was one she couldn't read.

Suddenly self-conscious, she lowered the pizza slice. "What service is that exactly?"

Matthew drew in a long breath and looked like he was debating what to tell her. There was only one thing she wanted. The truth. It might be hypocritical of her not to have told him everything that she'd done to survive. She hadn't outright said that she had actually shot and killed some of Emmanuel's other victims, but she needed him to be honest with her.

"I like you, Grace. I know it's not appropriate given everything you've been through, but I can't help it. I really like you, and I want to be your friend, and when you're ready I'd like to be more than friends," he blurted out as though scared he'd lose his nerve.

Her breath whooshed out in a rush.

Had he really just said he liked her?

That he wanted to date her?

"I really do know my timing sucks," he added when she didn't say anything. "And I won't be offended if you tell me to get out and not come back. I'll be disappointed but I promise I'll understand."

"Disappointed, huh?"

"Definitely."

"Well," she dragged the word out, "considering you've brought me meals three times now I wouldn't want that. Matthew," she sighed and knew she had to tell him, "when I said I was responsible for some of the victim's deaths I meant that Emmanuel gave me a gun and told me to shoot them or he'd kill me. I wanted to shoot him so badly, but I was chained up and the key was in the other room, if I took him out, I was dead."

Instead of looking shocked at her admission he reached over and rested a hand on her knee, his fingers tracing absent circles. There was an understanding in his eyes that she didn't quite get.

"Grace, my dad walked out on me, my mom, and sister when I was four and my sister was eight. After that things were really rough. My mom did her best, worked three jobs, but we barely had enough to eat. When I was nine my mom met a guy, he wasn't rich, but he was well off and he opened up his home to us. My sister and I each had our own room, we had toys and clothes, and we never went to bed hungry. It was great. For a while. Then he started getting violent with my mom. He'd tell her she wasn't doing enough to keep up her looks, that she was looking old, letting herself go. He made her work out for hours every day, restricted what she could eat, picked out all her clothes for her. Then I started noticing he paid a lot of attention to my sister. I saw him coming out of her room late at night a few times and I knew. Bessie was only fifteen, he was forty-five, it was wrong. I told my mom but instead of being sickened at the thought of that man touching her daughter like I was, she was jealous. Bessie looked just like mom only younger. Mom tried to insist that Bessie date boys her own age and my stepfather started beating on her, worse than I'd ever seen, I thought she was dead. When he grabbed Bessie and dragged her toward the garage I panicked. I thought he was going to kidnap her and take her away, I knew it was only a matter of time before he started beating her like he did mom, killed her too. So, I got his gun and shot him. Killed him with a lucky shot to the heart."

Her heart pounded in her chest as she listened to Matthew's story, it ached for the little boy who had gone through so much. Without her even realizing it, she'd claimed his hand, entwined their fingers, and was clinging to it tightly. Matthew lifted their joined hands and touched a kiss to hers.

"So you see, Grace, I understand what you did and how it felt. You did what you had to do but you didn't like doing it. It changed something in you, left you with guilt you don't know how to deal with. But you did the right thing, the only thing you could do. I understand you in a way not many people can or will, and I want to be there for you. Not just to help you deal with it, but to see the joy on your face like this morning outside. I want to make you feel that way every day. I want to help you learn about happiness again, watch as you realize your own strength, learn everything there is to know about you. But I can wait, I can be patient, for as long as you need I'm happy to be just your friend."

Tears blurred her vision but didn't tumble down her cheeks, and she set the pizza down and leaned across the small table to touch a chaste kiss to his lips. "Thank you." The words didn't seem like enough for the peace he'd given her by truly understanding her, but for now they were all she had to offer.

CHAPTER
Four

July 9th
1:16 A.M.

Emmanuel couldn't decide if he was more angry or in pain.

Both were pretty high off the charts.

He'd twisted his knee jumping out the hospital room window and had a pretty nasty cut on his side from the glass. Then there were all the bumps and bruises. He felt like he'd been tossed into the back of a cement truck and spun around.

The bumps and bruises he couldn't do anything about. The wrecked knee was currently propped up on a pillow with an ice pack resting on it, but he was worried about the gash along his side. The wound was still bleeding sluggishly, the torn skin was jagged, and he knew there was a good chance infection would set in if he didn't close the gash.

First thing he'd done after fleeing the hospital was come back here and clean it out. He'd flushed it with warm, salty water and then slathered it with antibiotic cream and wrapped a bandage around his middle. At first, he'd hoped that was enough but every time he looked the bandage was stained red with his blood. Didn't matter how much pressure he applied, or how many times he bandaged it, or how many hours passed, the stupid wound wouldn't stop bleeding.

What he needed was a hospital, the gash obviously needed stitches. He had actually contemplated circling the hospital and going into the ER, but he'd garnered an audience with his stunt and had been worried someone would recognize him. So, he'd thought of driving to another hospital, but the fear that they might have alerted hospitals to be on the lookout for someone matching his description and with injuries consistent with a fall had stopped him from doing it.

He was on his own for this one.

Going to a hospital, even going to a clinic or a doctor, was too risky. There was no way he could allow the cops to get his real name. If they did it would be game over, so he was going to have to find a way to deal with his injury himself.

Maybe he could stitch himself.

It wouldn't be the first time he'd stitched someone, just the first time he'd done it to himself. Some of his games had gotten a little out of hand, and on more than one occasion he had tended to Grace's wounds. It didn't matter what test he gave her, what he put her through, she always managed to come out on top.

Emmanuel was starting to believe she was less human and more angel.

Salvation.

She was his salvation.

It was why he was so desperate to get her back, although he was pretty sure that was going to be next to impossible now. He'd been so careful at the hospital, making sure nobody—including the CCTV cameras—got a good look at him. He'd waited patiently until she was alone before making his move. He had hoped to be able to take her out of the hospital through the front door but been prepared to have to jump out the window. It was a high risk move but he was desperate, grabbing her at the hospital was easier than trying to figure out where she would be living and targeting her there.

But now they knew he wanted her back, they would be extra

cautious. It was unlikely she'd ever be alone until they apprehended him and without her steady, calming presence, he could already feel himself falling apart.

Didn't they understand that she was his only hope at redemption?

It was meant to be. If it wasn't, she would have failed before now.

How could she keep winning time after time, against different women, with different tests? The only explanation was that the Universe was giving him a second chance. A chance to save this time where he had failed so dismally in the past.

When he had started his lessons, he had never expected that one woman would keep winning. He thought they would all fail, that it was all women did, they failed and failed and failed.

But not Grace.

His Grace was a survivor.

She was the key.

He needed her.

"I need her," he screamed at the top of his lungs. No one would hear him, this place was soundproofed just like Mable White's house had been. He'd done it himself. When he'd gone into the building trade, he had never expected to need those skills for anything other than his job, and yet here he was. Those very skills had come in so handy, and now he not only had a successful business, but he was able to custom renovate houses to be exactly what he needed.

But they wouldn't find him here.

How could they?

It was just a fluke that they had found the last place, nothing that could happen twice, especially not when he had the Universe on his side.

Carefully levering himself out of bed, he staggered to the bathroom and removed the bandages. He'd stitch himself up and then he was going to have to do something to alleviate the ball of pressure sitting on his chest.

All that fear and guilt he had managed to stamp down and lock in a box while he had Grace in his possession was forcing its way back out. If he didn't deal with it, then it was going to consume him all over again.

Pulling out his first aid kit, fully equipped with several suture kits, he set about laying out what he would need. This wasn't going to be fun but knowing he could go and blow off a little steam afterward was definite motivation.

Opening up the kit, he doused his wound with saline before preparing the needle. It was an awkward angle, the wound running from just below his ribs on his right side, down to just above his hip, but it wasn't like there was any other option, so he gritted his teeth and began.

The first stab of the needle hurt a whole lot more than he thought it would and he cursed himself for not stocking local anesthetic. It had never been an issue before because he'd never had to do it on himself, and he'd looked at Grace handling pain as just another lesson.

But he couldn't hold back a howl as he pulled the threat tight and moved on to the second stich. How had Grace managed to not make a sound when he was stitching her up? She might have winced, but she'd never so much as grunted in pain the few times he'd had to put in sutures.

More proof that the woman was more angel than human.

The wound was long, at least six inches, and it seemed to hurt worse with each stitch he put in. By the time he got to the last one he was sweating, breathing heavily, his hands shaking so much he could hardly get the stitch in.

That was hell.

While he certainly didn't plan on getting banged up again, he was adding a stock of local anesthetic to his supplies. If he ever had to put sutures in a wound of Grace's again, there was no way he could do it without getting queasy if he knew first-hand the pain he was inflicting on her.

Bandaging himself to protect the stitches, he sighed in relief that it was done and sagged down onto the toilet for a moment to catch his breath. He couldn't go far in his current condition, but he didn't need to. There was a woman across the street who looked similar to Grace. For tonight she could take his angel's place and help him banish the bad thoughts and feelings that wanted to destroy him.

Smiling now, Emmanuel shoved to his feet, cleaned up, then dressed in a loose-fitting t-shirt and jeans, careful to keep them slung low on his hips so they didn't add pressure to his wound. Then he swallowed a couple of painkillers and a glass of water and headed downstairs. He felt a little lightheaded, no doubt due to the blood he had lost, but he didn't care, he needed to kill.

Despite what the cops thought, he wasn't a killer. The only life he had ever ended himself was the woman the other night. The women he had tried to help had lost their lives as a result of the lessons, not his fault, the Universe was the one responsible for that. Grace had killed the others, not him.

But this morning, he was going to claim his second soul. He was sure the Universe would understand. After all, it was either kill his neighbor or give in to the guilt and take his own life, and he couldn't do that until he had his Grace back.

9:12 A.M.

"What are we doing here?" Rylla asked.

Matthew didn't answer his partner for a moment, his attention fixed on the naked body of Natalie Potter. The woman's body had been discovered early this morning when a colleague who she carpooled with came to pick her up, discovered the front door open, and Natalie lying dead at the bottom of the stairs.

The medical examiner was yet to rule out an accidental death, and while Matthew agreed there was the slimmest of chances that the woman had slipped and fallen, he thought it was pretty unlikely. It wasn't just the fact that the bruises closely resembled a beating, or that it wasn't likely a fit that a twenty-nine-year-old woman would break her neck in a fall down the stairs, it was the tattoo.

"Matt? What are you thinking? I would have thought you would have wanted to focus on Grace's case, given that the two of you have grown close. So why are we here at the scene of a suspicious death? I mean, I agree this poor woman was probably beaten to death, but it isn't our case," Rylla said.

Nothing was more important to him than finding Emmanuel and

making sure Grace was safe. They'd bonded last night when he'd told her what happened with his family and how he knew what it was like to take a life. In his career as a cop, he'd had to kill to protect himself and others twice, and while both of those times had affected him deeply, it was nothing like the guilt he carried from killing his stepfather.

Grace got that.

Got it in a way not many others could.

At least she had the support of her family. Even if they weren't aware of the fact she had to shoot some of Emmanuel's victims to survive, Matthew knew there was no way they would turn their backs on her.

Unlike his family.

His mother had been furious that her meal ticket was dead, and they were back out on the streets. His sister had believed she was in love with their stepfather and had been devastated at his death. At just eleven years old, he'd been handed over to social services by his mother who had disappeared with his sister, and never once looked back. Matthew had spent the rest of his childhood in various foster homes until he aged out. He'd put himself through college, joined the police force, worked hard to become a detective and get a coveted spot on the homicide squad. But he hadn't been able to outrun the feelings of guilt, betrayal, and abandonment. It was why he was so determined not to let Grace blame herself for things she had no control over.

"Maybe this should be our case," he said as he crouched beside the body and pointed to a small tattoo on the woman's ankle, proof as far as he was concerned that this was murder and not an accident. "See this?"

Rylla squatted beside him. "A mouse tattoo? What are you thinking?"

Standing, he walked away from the body and outside to stand on the front porch. The day was already warming up, it was going to be a hot one. Summer had been slow to get off the ground but now that it had warmed up, it seemed like the hot weather was here to stay. The sky above was a clear, deep blue that reminded him of Grace's eyes, and he was glad that this year she would be able to enjoy the summer. In fact, he was going to make sure she enjoyed it.

"Grace said that Emmanuel had a thing for fables. The tortoise and the hare, the ant and the grasshopper, the gnat and the bull, the lion and the mouse, so last night I got to thinking. After I left the hospital for the night, I went by the station and started searching through cold cases. We know that Emmanuel didn't bury the bodies at Mable White's house because hers was the only body we found there which means he had to dispose of them some other way. I started with cold cases, but there might be some where someone was charged for the murder as well, we'll have to look into it."

"Look into what exactly?" Rylla asked.

"Tattoos. If the fables were as important to Emmanuel as Grace said they were, and we have no reason to disbelieve her, we've both seen the basement, then I got to wondering if he would have marked the bodies somehow. I searched cold cases, cross referencing for any female victim in her twenties or thirties, since Grace said all the women were fairly close in age to her, that had a tattoo, specifically one of his favorite fables. I focused just on the ones Grace mentioned, hare, tortoise, ant, grasshopper, gnat, bull, lion, and mouse, and I found a dozen hits. A few of the women had been shot, a couple drowned, one had been beaten, another stabbed, but all of them had a recent tattoo on their ankle. In the case notes it said families and friends all reported that the victims did not have any tattoos."

"So, he does them himself."

"That would be my guess. Gives us another avenue of tracking this guy down."

"How do we know that these women were his victims though?"

"Tattoos were done postmortem. All animals in what we know are his favorite fables, all unsolved murders over the last six years, all women in the age range he targets. We don't know for sure, but I think we should start looking into their murders, see if we can connect them to Grace's case." Matthew knew in his gut that these women were victims of Emmanuel's sick lessons, and he knew that his partner would support him. He hoped they could find proof to link them to Emmanuel. But even if they couldn't, the man would be facing life in prison for Grace's abduction and torture alone. Still, he didn't want to give a judge any reason whatsoever to ever let Emmanuel walk free, so the more crimes they could charge him with the better.

"Why did no one else ever link the cases?"

"Dump sites were different and they weren't all killed the same way. Different jurisdictions, a couple had violent exes who looked like they could have done it, there just wasn't enough for someone to notice that these women's cases might be linked, even with the tattoos which you would have to know to look into. I only had the hunch because of what we learned from Grace. Without her mentioning the fables there would be no reason to think random tattoos meant anything at all. For all the cops on those cases knew, the women had gone and gotten them voluntarily before they were abducted and just not told anyone."

"Natalie Potter has one, so you think he killed her last night. That's way outside his MO."

"I know, but yesterday wasn't a normal day for him. He needs Grace back, it was a massive risk to try to get her out of the hospital. If he tried, he's desperate. Having his attempts foiled would have sent him off the deep end. I'm guessing he lives somewhere around here or he just happened to catch sight of Natalie. She looks a lot like Grace, same blonde curls, same blue eyes."

"She was a substitute. He took out his anger at not being able to get his hands on the real thing on her."

"When I heard about the case, saw a picture of the victim, I just knew. Then when I saw the tattoo, I knew I was right. He's going off script, killed this one himself, there's no telling what he's going to do next."

"Except make another attempt on Grace," Rylla said softly.

His chest constricted at his partner's words even though he already knew that. Grace wasn't safe, never would be unless they could get Emmanuel off the streets. "Yeah, that's a given."

"How is he choosing them? We're going to have to go through the list of victims you found and find out where their lives intersect because wherever he finds them, that's how we're going to find him."

"We can take the list of other victims to Grace later, see if she recognizes any of them. Once she gets names or she knows some of the places that the others frequent, gyms, restaurants, grocery stores, banks, pharmacies, then she might realize that she goes there too. We have to find him, Rylla. We *have* to. If we don't, not only will Grace never be safe, but neither will any woman who resembles her, or any woman who crosses Emmanuel's path. He's never going to stop, whatever is fueling him is too strong. He's going to keep killing until he's caught or he's killed."

Last night Grace had kissed him, and she hadn't been thrown by him telling her that he liked her and hoped one day they might be more than friends. Matthew hadn't thought he would ever meet a woman who he connected with like he did with Grace, hadn't even been sure if he deserved to find happiness in the arms of a woman after the life he'd taken. But Grace got to him, had lodged herself inside his heart, and he could see himself falling in love with her.

There was no way he was letting her fall into the hands of a madman a second time.

～

10:34 A.M.

"I think I'm going to change my masters," Grace announced as they drove toward the nursing home where her mom resided. She'd been released from the hospital about thirty minutes ago, and it felt so good to finally be free of that place. While it was by no means anywhere close to the prison she had been living in for the last five and a half years, it was a different kind of prison, like being trapped in limbo, not really able to move forward.

Well, now the future was what she was focusing on.

She wanted to get back to her studies, she wanted to find a job, and get her own place. She was even just looking forward to a shopping trip so she could go and buy her own things. Not that she didn't appreciate Ali and Laynie for lending her some clothes, or Jem and Laynie allowing her to live with them until she got her life sorted out, but she wanted to be her own person again. In charge of her own life, making her own decisions, and working toward the future she wanted.

Perhaps she was still being wildly naïve—a trait she thought had been forced out of her as Emmanuel's plaything—but she didn't want what had happened to her to define her or the rest of her life.

"What?" Jem asked, throwing her a quick glance before returning his gaze to the road.

"I was going to follow you into criminal psychology, I always thought it would be cool to understand why bad guys do the things they do, and I wanted to help make the world a safer place. I still think that what you do is so important, and I know better than most just how much evil there is in the world, but it's not what I want to do with my life. I'd rather go for a straight psychology degree, specialize in working with victims." While Grace couldn't remember a time she didn't want to be like her big brother, now she realized that her unique experience meant she could help people heal from trauma. A psychologist had come to speak with her at the hospital, and while the middle-aged woman was lovely and very empathetic, there was no way she could truly understand what it felt like to be snatched away, locked up, and forced to endure hell with no signs of end in sight.

But Grace could help others like her because she was one of them.

That was when she'd known she no longer wanted to focus on criminals but on the victims whose lives they forever changed.

If she hunted criminals, she would be stuck in a cycle where every time they caught one another would pop up to take their place. But helping victims meant changing someone's world for the better.

"It's not that I don't think that's a good idea, Gracie, and I know for a fact you would be amazing at it, but I don't think now is the time to be making any big life decisions," Jem said.

"Why not? It feels like the perfect time to be reevaluating what I want to get out of life."

"Because you've just lived through a major trauma."

"Exactly. I know what it's like to think that I'm not going to ever have a normal life, and now that I'm safe and alive I don't want to waste time. I was thinking if I called up my old college, I could see what I needed to do to register for the fall semester. And I still have contacts, I'm sure I could find a job in the field based on my degree, that way I could work, get my own place, and work on getting my masters." She could also see about letting things develop between her and Matthew, but she didn't say that out loud. If Jem was freaking out about her wanting to go back to school, he would certainly lose it if he knew she was considering dating already.

"Why don't you just give yourself a little time to breathe first," Jem said in a somewhat condescending tone that totally rankled.

"Because I know what it's like to not be able to breathe. What good is sitting around your house doing nothing going to do?"

"It will give you time to get your feet beneath you," he said as he pulled into the parking lot for the nursing home and parked in the first available space.

Grace unbuckled her seatbelt, climbed out of the car, planted her hands on her hips, and leaned down to peer at her big brother. "I have my feet beneath me, see? And I'm standing all steady, no wobbling. I want to get my life back. Why can't you understand that?"

"Oh, honey, I understand that, I do," Jem assured her as he also climbed out of the car and rounded it to stand beside her. "But what you went through is horrific and instead of confronting it and dealing with it you're trying to avoid it, pretend it never happened."

"So, what's wrong with that?" she asked defensively. She knew this was the right path for her. She needed to be doing something with her life. For five and a half years she'd sat around a room, locked inside it unable to leave with nothing to do but think of the horrible things she'd endured. She wasn't living that way anymore.

"It doesn't work," Jem said gently. "You have to process what happened before you can deal with it."

"I can process and work on getting my life back at the same time," she said. This was exactly why she knew she wanted to focus on victims and not criminals. Jem didn't get it. He was trying and she loved him for it, but he didn't understand.

"We'll make some calls, see what we need to do to get you enrolled," he agreed.

Her eyes widened with surprise. "Really?"

"If it's what you want."

"Please don't sound so enthusiastic about it," she said with an eye roll. Her brother's tone couldn't be less happy with her plan if he tried.

Jem laughed. "Gracie, I'm happy about it. I am. I know you will make an amazing therapist, and no one would be better equipped to help victims of crime. You're smart, empathetic, have a great ability to read people, and while I think you would make an excellent profiler, I agree you would be fantastic helping people deal with trauma. That's not what I meant. I just don't want you to make a decision you'll regret later because you're so insistent to try to move on with your life."

"I know what I'm doing, Jem," she assured him.

"Then I'll help you make it happen." He leaned down and kissed her forehead before taking her hand and leading her across the parking lot and inside the facility.

It was exactly as she remembered it, same light gray paint on the walls, same dark wooden floorboards, same paintings on the wall. Nothing had changed, it was like the last five and a half years hadn't happened.

At least that was how Grace felt until they stepped inside her mom's room, and she laid eyes on her mother for the first time in so long. The last time she'd seen her mom was the weekend before she'd been kidnapped. She'd been twenty-two then, busy balancing studying for her masters in criminal psychology with working part time at a local bookstore, with volunteering to get as much experience in her field as she could. Then there were friends, and when she had time the occasional boyfriend. She hadn't visited her mother as often as she should have, something she now deeply regretted.

Her mom had aged so much. Back then, it had only been a few months since the stroke. Her mom had been determined to regain as much function as she could even though the doctors said she would never walk or talk again, never feed herself, and never be able to do anything but lie in a bed, trapped inside her body.

While she had been trapped in Emmanuel's house Grace had worried that her only daughter's abduction would make her mom give up, but as her mom's eyes moved toward the door, and she saw the spark of fire still in them, she knew that she shouldn't have worried.

Like mother like daughter, her mom was a fighter, and had obviously instilled that same determination in Grace. It was the only way she could have survived for so long as Emmanuel's prisoner.

Grace flew across the room and wrapped her arms around her mom, careful not to mess with the tubes and wires that kept her mom alive and monitored her vital signs. She pressed her face against her neck, and even though her mom couldn't move, couldn't hug or hold her, Grace felt her love as surely as if she could.

There was no place on earth like your mother's arms, no matter how big you were.

~

8:49 P.M.

"Okay, Matt, I think we should call it a night."

Matthew glanced up at his partner's voice, but he shook his head. They were working on a list of names of potential victims. In addition to the dozen he'd found yesterday, they'd been able to add another six to that list. Plus, another three where someone had been charged and convicted of a murder of a woman they knew, where the victim also had a recently acquired tattoo on her ankle. While he intended to speak with Grace and find out if she could positively identify the women as Emmanuel's victims, for now, he was working the theory that they were and he and Rylla were trying to simultaneously look for more and try to find any links between them.

He didn't want to go home for the night until he had something concrete.

The drive to find Emmanuel was unlike anything he had experienced on any other case. He was always driven, you had to be to do this kind of work, but this was something else. This growing thing between him and Grace was consuming him, and he had to bring her the peace she needed to be able to live the rest of her life to the fullest.

"Matt." Rylla rolled her chair over from her desk to beside him. "I know you want to fix this for Grace, I remember how I felt when my sister was abducted, how badly I wanted to find her, so I get where you're coming from. But that doesn't mean running yourself into the ground is the answer. You like Grace, it's obvious, I'm guessing since you've been hanging out with her a bit that she likes you too. You want to be her hero, ride in on your white horse to save her, but remember there's more than one way to save someone. Maybe Grace needs you just to be there more than she needs you to solve this case."

Not giving him a chance to reply, she stood, squeezed his shoulder, then returned her chair to her desk and gathered her things.

Matthew sat there watching her walk away, her footsteps echoing in the mostly empty bullpen. Everyone else had gone home for the night except for Heidi, who was in her office, working late like she always did. The drive to close Grace's case hadn't diminished, and her safety depended on Emmanuel being caught, but maybe there was a little truth to what Rylla had said.

With a sigh, he shoved back from the desk, shutting down his laptop for the night. It would still be here in the morning, and his stomach chose that moment to grumble loudly reminding him he hadn't eaten since lunch.

Grabbing his cell phone and keys, he headed for the parking lot. He'd stop off, grab something to eat on the way home. If Grace had still been in the hospital, he would have been tempted to take something around to hang out with her for a while, but now that she was at her brother's house he couldn't do that.

Would that change things between them?

Not that there *was* much between them, but Grace had kissed him, and she hadn't said she wasn't interested when he'd told her he liked her. In fact, the way she'd admitted to being coerced into shooting some of Emmanuel's victims said the opposite. She'd been protecting her heart, giving him an out which had to mean that she was interested too.

Now that she was home, ready to rebuild her life, would she decide there was room in hers for him?

He'd just climbed into his car when his cell phone rang. He debated ignoring it. There wasn't anyone he wanted to talk to, and besides, all his friends were married now, had kids, or were thinking of starting families. Unless they had made plans, he didn't usually hear from them after nine.

Had Emmanuel struck again?

The fear that he'd made another attempt at snatching Grace was the reason he pulled his cell out of his pocket. It was an unknown caller, and yet he accepted the call even though it was likely a scammer, usually the only calls he got from someone not one of his saved contacts.

"Hello?" he said as he closed the car door and turned on the engine.

"Matthew?"

"Grace?"

"It's me. Jem got me a cell phone, it's way fancier than the one I had when I was taken. I asked him for your number, I hope that's okay." She sounded tentative, almost shy, but he was grinning like an idiot, too bad she couldn't see that. Grace had tracked him down, she'd only left the hospital this morning, and yet she'd already got a phone and called him.

"It's more than okay, I'm so glad to hear from you."

"I wasn't sure if you'd want to. I mean, I know what you said earlier, about how you ... you know ... liked me, and I don't think I'm ready for anything right now, not a relationship anyway, but I do need a friend, and I'd like to get to know you better. I know it's a lot to ask of you because I don't know when I'm going to be ready, and I can't expect you to wait, but ..."

But she was asking him to wait, and it was everything he wanted to hear.

No way had he expected her to be so upfront with asking him to wait for her, but he was so glad she wasn't afraid to ask for what she needed because over the coming days, weeks, and months as she healed from her ordeal, she was going to need to reach out to her support system.

A system he was honored to be part of.

"Grace, it is more than okay. It's not too much to ask at all. I told you I like you but that I knew my timing sucked. I'll wait for as long as it takes."

There was a long pause, but he could hear her breathing on the other end of the line. "What if I'm never ready?"

"Then I'll have a best friend I'll never walk away from," he replied without hesitation. It was true. Would he be disappointed if things never progressed any further between them, yeah, he would, but if the only way to be part of Grace's life was as a friend, then he would be the best friend he could be to her.

Her breath whooshed out, and he could tell she was relieved.

"Thank you. I don't want to make you wait, I promise, I'm not trying to play games. Jem and I made some calls today, I'm hoping to start school in the fall, and I'm going to go looking for a job soon. I'm determined to get my life back, Emmanuel isn't stealing anything more from me. I'd like you to be part of that future, but I just need to get my feet beneath me first."

"You don't need to explain yourself, Grace, I understand. Really. You have a lot on your plate, it's okay to focus on yourself first. I think it's great that you're so determined to rebuild, and I think you going back to college is a wonderful idea, but, Grace, I hope you're taking care of yourself too. Are you seeing a therapist?" Since they seemed to be on an honesty kick when it came to each other, he didn't want to beat around the bush. It was important for her to rebuild her life, he knew it was because she'd had no control over it for the last five and a half years. Now she was exerting that control again, but she had to take care of her mental health as well.

"Jem insisted. I like her but she doesn't get it, not like you," she added softly.

So it was the shooting of the other victims weighing the heaviest on her mind. While he was glad he could help her, he wasn't a substitute for a real psychologist, he couldn't provide the support she needed. "You know I'm not going anywhere, and I'm here any time you need to talk, day or night, but I want you to promise me something."

"You want me to promise to keep seeing the therapist."

"Would that be so bad?"

Grace sighed. "No, I guess not. I'm just being stubborn. I was a psychology major you know, I was going to go into criminal psychology, like Jem, but I changed my mind, I want to help victims, people like me."

"I couldn't think of anyone who would do a better job of that than you."

"I can make a difference in people's lives," she said softly.

"Yeah, you can, sweetheart." Matthew couldn't think of anyone better qualified to guide victims through trauma than Grace Bennett.

"So, you sound like you're in your car. Are you just leaving work?"

Grace asked, and he could tell she was ready to move on from the deep stuff.

"Yep. Was just getting into the car when you called. I was going to stop off and grab some dinner on the way home."

"Do you want me to go?"

Putting the cell on speakerphone, he stuck it in the cupholder and put the car in reverse. "Nope. What I want is to learn everything there is about Grace Bennett."

"Everything?" she asked, and he could hear the smile in her voice.

"Everything, so get talking."

CHAPTER
Five

July 10th
11:04 A.M.

"Snap," Grace said as she slapped her hand down on top of the pile of cards. "I win again." While it wasn't the most difficult of games, it had been her favorite as a kid, and she had woken in a nostalgic mood. They'd already made her favorite m&m waffles for breakfast, then Elijah and Ali had come over and now they were all hanging out, playing card games, talking, and laughing. It was almost like old times.

"You do know that we're letting you win, right?" Elijah asked with an eye roll.

Grace just grinned. "I know, you guys always used to let me win." It had been one of her favorite things about being the baby of the family. She knew she had been spoiled, so used to getting her own way that she'd come to expect it, at least with her family. When she was with her friends and boyfriends, she tried to never act entitled. It was one thing for her big brothers to spoil her, but another for others to do it, she would never expect that. Instead, she tried to do the opposite, look for little things to do to make others smile. Just like her family let her win at games, or choose what movie they went to because they wanted her to be happy, she wanted to share that joy.

Never once had she doubted she was extremely lucky to be born to parents who adored her even if she was an unplanned surprise. Her parents had both been cops, but they'd always made sure that she was well taken care of even with their crazy schedules. Her extended family of big brothers, and Laynie and Ali and their parents, had always been there to take care of her, and she'd always felt loved, respected, and supported. So many people didn't have what she'd been blessed with, and she'd wanted to do what she could to let others know they were cared about.

Now she wanted to help others realize their strength.

"Want to play again?" she asked.

The others groaned, making her laugh. "No. More. Snap." Ali said, over enunciating each word and making them all laugh again.

This was so nice. Just hanging out together, she'd missed moments like this and thought she would never get to experience them again, but here she was. Was it possible to be any more grateful than she was in this moment?

"Fine," she said dramatically as she got off the floor and flopped onto the sofa next to Laynie. "If you don't want to play anymore you guys can help me choose a puppy."

"A puppy?" Jem asked.

"Or maybe an older dog. If you guys don't want one living here I understand, and I'll wait until I get my own place." She knew that Jem and Laynie loved dogs. They'd had one when she had been taken although it had passed away while she was gone. But she also wasn't just going to assume that they'd be happy with her getting one while she was here.

"Gracie, you know we're happy for you to stay here as long as you need," Laynie said.

"I know, but I want my life back." Grace was pretty sure that if they had their way Jem and Laynie would keep her here forever. They were struggling to heal too, and they wanted to keep her close. She couldn't imagine how hard it had been for them knowing she was gone, knowing she was in trouble, but not being able to find her. It wasn't that she wanted to hurt them, but at the same time she had to start living. She had to try to get back the years she had lost, she wanted her independence, and staying here too long would make it harder to leave. This place would become her safety blanket but that would also make it a different type of prison. A nicer one, one where she would be loved and looked after, but also one where she wouldn't be free.

"All right," Jem said. She could tell he was holding back, but she loved and respected that her family were trying to put her first. "What kind of dog are you thinking of getting?"

"Big," she answered immediately. While Grace knew that she wanted to find a job and then get her own place, get her independence back, she also knew that living alone was going to be hard. It would take time for her not to be afraid in a house on her own, given she was abducted from her home that night. But she was determined to dissect every single one of her fears and overcome them.

And maybe she wouldn't be living alone for long.

Maybe she'd be having a roommate in the not-too-distant future.

A two legged one, not the furry companion she was looking for now.

Last night, talking to Matthew she'd had so much fun. Knowing he was willing to wait for her made her even more determined to get herself together. Grace knew her family thought she was living in denial, that she wasn't processing what had happened, that she was holding it together too well, but they were wrong. She was healing the best way she knew how and that was to focus on the future, to live for herself and the victims, to do the very thing that she'd fought for all these years.

She had to live.

"What about a protection dog?" Elijah suggested. "That could be the best of both worlds. You get a furry friend, and someone to help you feel safe, and maybe we won't worry about you as much if we know that you have a big, mean looking dog watching your back."

"I like that idea," she agreed. She'd been thinking of getting a puppy, but now that her brother suggested it, she liked the idea of getting a protection dog. It really would make her feel safer but still give her a warm, furry body to hold onto when she needed a reminder that she was safe and no longer alone. "How do I go about finding a protection dog?"

"I have a few contacts. Leave it with me and I'll get back to you on it," Laynie said.

Grace reached for a cookie from the plate on the coffee table and noticed the others were exchanging glances. "What's up?"

"Tell her, Jem," Laynie said, taking her husband's hand.

"I found you a job," Jem announced.

Her eyes lit up. "You did? Where?"

"It's a clinic run by a friend. She specializes in victims of trauma and she's looking for a new receptionist. She knows who you are, what you've been through, what you've studied, and what you want to study when you go back to school next semester. She's happy for you to work with her so long as you keep up the office work as well," Jem told her.

This was perfect. A dog, a job, and a chance to get meaningful experience in the field she wanted to work in. It was everything she wanted, a normal life. A job meant she could get her own place, and doing something that mattered might heal her heart. The constant companionship of a dog would help her when bad moments hit, and maybe a romantic relationship wasn't as far away as she thought it was.

Grace threw her arms around both Jem and Laynie because she knew without his wife giving him a nudge, her brother would have given in to the need to keep her close, clip her wings without meaning to, but nonetheless it would hamper her ability to learn to fly again. "Thank you," she whispered, "I know that was hard for you."

"I want to keep you close, Gracie. We all do. I want you to stay here forever, where I can see you every day, where I can know for sure you're okay. I want to follow you around and never let you out of my sight. But you've proven over and over again that you're a fighter, that you're strong, and that you know what you're doing. So, we're all here for you, to support you, help you get your feet back underneath you, help you get back what you lost," Jem said.

"I love you all so much." She squeezed hard then moved to the other couch to huge Elijah and Ali. "I missed you all so much, and part of me wants to stay right here, letting you take care of me now. But that would be giving up and I didn't do it when I was with Emmanuel and I'm not going to do it now. But you guys have to know that you're the reason that I'm still here, you taught me to be strong. I did what I know you would do if you were taken. Now you're helping me in a different way. Helping me go back to school, find a job, and get a dog. I want you to teach me to shoot as well and some self-defense moves. If Emmanuel comes after me, I want to be able to protect myself. I'm not giving up, not ever. Not when I have so much to live for."

Making amends for the lives she took, helping other victims, spending time with her family, and Matthew. He made her laugh, helped her relax, and understood her in a way she had been afraid no one ever could.

～

2:18 P.M.

"Zara and Amanda went to the same gym, but none of the other women did," Matthew said, setting the photos of those two victims side by side.

"And Darla and Rosie lived on the same street, but nobody else lived in that area," Rylla added.

"Frances used the same bank as Amanda, but none of the other women used it."

"Frances, Billie, and Jean all used the same dry cleaner."

"Tamara and Natasha both go to the same doctor, and Amelia used the physiotherapist who works out of the same building after she injured herself at Taekwondo. And Rosie and Billie use the dentist who's also in the same building." That was the biggest link they'd found so far. Five of their twenty-one victims all went to the same facility even though they used different parts of the building. They'd be going through everybody who worked there, was a patient there, or any contractors who frequented the place looking for anyone who might be a suspect. Because they had Grace and Barbara Lack, they would be able to get the women to ID any suspect they got which meant they wouldn't waste time chasing down leads that didn't pan out.

But they couldn't ask Grace and Barbara Lack to look at photos of every man in his late twenties to mid-thirties that lived in the city, that was just too wide a suspect pool. Once they narrowed things down though they'd have the two women look at their list and see if any of the men were Emmanuel.

At least they had a list of Emmanuel's victims to work with. Even though he hadn't wanted to ruin the fun he and Grace were having talking on the phone last night before wishing her sweet dreams and saying goodnight, he'd asked if he could send her a list of potential victims. She'd agreed and first thing this morning he'd sent her pictures of thirty women. She'd come back to him with a list of twenty-one that she recognized as being in Emmanuel's house, but some of the bodies with tattoos were from before Grace had been kidnapped so they knew he had other victims even if they couldn't prove it.

"None of the other victims have any connections there though," Rylla said, sounding as frustrated as he felt. They had been working on this all day and even though they'd been able to link some of the victims together, they hadn't found one place where all twenty-one—twenty-three if they included Grace and Barbara Lack—women connected.

Without that connection it was next to impossible to find the man.

They'd already eliminated the easy route the first day by checking into any men with the name Emmanuel, but there were none who matched the description they had. The man was using an alias, likely laying low in the house of another elderly woman he'd killed. If they couldn't find the link, they might not be able to locate Emmanuel. If they couldn't locate the man, then he was going to keep coming after Grace until they caught him or he got her.

"We have a few who worked in the same building, a couple who went to the same college, a couple use the same supermarket, a couple ran the same track at the local park, but there's nowhere that all of them went. Nothing that links them all together," Rylla continued.

"There is. There has to be something that links them."

"There doesn't have to be," his partner reminded him. "He could have picked houses at random."

Matthew shook his head. "Too risky. He needed to know who was in there. Every single one of his victims lived alone. He had to know that. The abductions were all smooth, he broke in, knocked them out, took them and got out of there. No witnesses, no fingerprints left behind. He knew what he was doing. There is no way someone who was that careful, put that much planning into it, just picked a house at random and took whoever was inside. What if he chose a house and found a man lived there, or a couple, or a whole family?"

"He could pick a house, wait to see who goes in?" Rylla suggested.

"I can't see him playing things loose. This guy went to the effort of finding a house that was not connected to him in any way, got the owner out of the way, and repurposed it to suit his needs. He's stayed off the radar, we got no hits on his fingerprints or DNA, so he has no criminal record. This guy is smart and careful, he's not going to leave it up to chance. He sees them somewhere, I know he does."

"Then we're at an impasse for now. I don't know how we're going to find him if we can't find the link."

Frustration surged through him. They knew what this man looked like and they had his DNA and his fingerprints. They knew where he had tortured and killed his victims, all of said victims' bodies had been found. They knew how he killed them and the why—although not in much detail—and yet they were no closer to finding him than if they had nothing.

It felt like their only option was to sit back and wait to see what Emmanuel's next move was going to be.

The problem with that was he knew what that next move would be.

Grace.

By going after her once already he'd made his intentions clear. He wanted her back, and if he was willing to chance a high-risk abduction by going after her while she was in the hospital, then he was desperate. Desperate enough that he'd gone and killed someone who looked like Grace just hours after the foiled kidnapping.

Matthew straightened, looking up from the photos covering the conference table. "Natalie Potter."

"What about her?" Rylla asked, rubbing the back of her neck as she sunk into her chair.

"We both agree she looks like Grace, right?"

"Right."

"And with the tattoo of the mouse on her ankle, the same place every single one of his other victims had a tattoo, we agree that its likely Natalie was killed by Emmanuel, right?"

"Right."

"Given the timeframe, so soon after Grace was nearly grabbed, we agree that it was Emmanuel lashing out, working out his anger at not getting what he wanted, right?"

"Right. Where are you going with this?"

"Just talking it through," he told Rylla. "So, we have a woman killed by a serial killer, right after he failed to get what he wanted. This victim looks just like the woman he tried and failed to get his hands on, so how did he find her?"

Rylla looked at him for a moment, then a spark lit in her green eyes as she realized what he was saying. "The attempted abduction of Grace was around four thirty in the afternoon, time of death for Natalie Potter was around two in the morning. That's less than twelve hours later. She lives approximately a thirty-minute drive from the hospital. It would have taken him a while to get to his car, witnesses said they saw him run off down the street. He was injured, but there was no blood other than Natalie's at the crime scene which meant he had to either go somewhere to receive treatment for his wounds or treat them himself. Let's say he needed at least a couple of hours to do that, meaning he had ten hours or less to find Natalie."

"Or he didn't have to find her." Matthew knew he was onto something here, he could feel it. "That's not a lot of time for him to happen across her. We need to find out what Natalie did that last afternoon she was alive. Make note of everywhere she went so we can check out each location, but I'm thinking he already knew Natalie. Emmanuel was angry, he needed to lash out, he was also hurt, he couldn't just go wandering around. And what are the chances he'd come across someone who looked so similar to her?"

"It would be a big risk to stay out in the open, dozens of people saw him jump out the window and run off," Rylla agreed. "It's much more likely he would have tried to lay low."

"Exactly. So, he already knew Natalie. He went to her specifically because she looked like Grace, she was as close to the real thing as he was going to be able to get his hands on any time soon. We need to speak with Natalie's family, find out everything we can about her because this guy knows her. She wasn't one of his victims, so she doesn't fit whatever he's looking for in the women he wants to teach lessons to, she's part of his regular life. If we look into Natalie's life, we'll find this guy."

∼

5:33 P.M.

Grace looked up from her video game when she heard the doorbell ring. A glance at the clock told her it was just after half past five and she realized she'd been playing the adorably cute Animal Crossing New Horizons game for almost four hours. She'd gotten so engrossed in choosing a name for her character and island, then choosing the perfect spot for her house, and learning DIYs and selling things to make Bells, that she had completely lost track of time.

The doorbell rang again, and she glanced around. She was alone in the living room, but she knew there was no way her family would have left her alone, they were far less ready to let her out of their sights than she was to be out of said sights. Elijah and Ali had left after lunch to go to work. She wasn't sure if Laynie was still home, but she knew Jem had taken a leave of absence to be around for her so he was here somewhere.

"Jem, doorbell," she called out, assuming he'd ordered dinner. She was definitely going through a takeout phase, basically bingeing on all the foods she hadn't eaten in so long. She was also overdoing it a little on the ice cream and KitKats which were her very favorite chocolate bar. But the way Grace figured it she'd definitely earned herself a few treats.

"Can you get it?"

"Why can't you get it?" She was all comfortable, curled up in a corner of the sofa, her snacks set out around her.

"Gracie, get the door, please."

"But I'm playing," she said in a voice that was dangerously close to a whine.

"Gracie." That tone she recognized from when she was a kid. It was Jem's exasperated voice, and she knew he wasn't getting the door.

"I don't know what you're doing that you can't get it," she muttered under her breath, but she wasn't really mad, and there was a smile on her lips as she remembered fun times playing video games with her brothers, and Ali and Laynie when she was younger. She'd gone through a huge Mario Kart phase and had spent literally hundreds of hours practicing then challenged her brothers to a race. She'd actually managed to beat them for real and she'd been thrilled. Beating two big brothers who were fifteen years older than you wasn't something you did often. At least not beating them for real.

When she opened the front door, she was surprised to see Matthew standing there. He was dressed in jeans that hugged his legs, and a white t-shirt that left little to the imagination. She could see every line of sculpted muscle, and her cheeks pinked as she realized just how attracted to him she was. It was not at all what she had expected, when she'd opened her eyes to find a cop hovering over her in the room where she had spent almost every day of the last five and a half years.

Then again, she hadn't been expecting to find someone who understood what she'd gone through. Her heart was still breaking for the little boy who had suffered so much, sacrificed so much to save his mother and sister, only to be shunned and abandoned for it.

"Matthew, this is a surprise."

"A good one I hope."

"The fact I'm grinning like an idiot isn't enough of a clue?" she teased. "What are you doing here?"

"I came to bring you these." He held out something even better than flowers, a whole stack of KitKats in every flavor that existed. "I heard you have a bit of a KitKat obsession at the moment."

"Not at the moment," she said as she greedily took the candy bars. "I *always* have an obsession with KitKats."

"I'll have to remember that."

There was heat in his eyes and a promise in his voice. She's been up front and honest with him about her concerns she might never be ready to give him what he wanted, but the very fact that he'd taken it in stride and told her he'd wait like it was the easiest thing in the world had her way more ready than she'd have thought.

"You didn't come all this way just to bring me chocolate. Why are you here?" Not that she wasn't thrilled to see him, but she assumed he'd come by for a purpose and wondered if he had more questions about the case. Of course, she would answer anything he asked, nobody wanted Emmanuel caught more than she did, but she wanted him to come for her not just for the case.

"I heard through the grapevine that you wanted to learn to shoot, and I thought I'd take you to the range, give you a lesson."

"Really?" Grace would have guessed Elijah, or maybe Ali or Laynie, would have wanted to teach her to shoot, not that she was complaining. An excuse to spend more time with Matthew? She'd jump all over that.

"Yep. Unless you don't want to." The uncertainty in his gaze made her want to smooth it away, reassure him. Grace had always been a fixer. Even though she had been spoiled and was a typical baby of the family, she had always been driven to help people. She's helped out around the house when her dad's health started to decline, looked after her mom after the stroke until she was abducted, helped friends at school however she could. The sight of someone in pain made her hurt too.

"No, of course I want to," she said quickly, and the smile he shot her made her stomach go all warm and tingly. "I just need to change, you can come in if you want, it won't take me long."

"I'll wait here," he told her.

Leaving the door open, Grace hurried into the kitchen where she found Jem sitting at the table. She went right to him, threw her arms around his neck, and hugged him, then kissed his cheek. "Thank you."

"It's not what I expected, but you seem to like him, to trust him. If I'm being selfish, I want you to come to me for comfort, for help, but I can't be selfish, not now. If he's what you need then I won't ever stand in the way."

"I love you, Jem."

"Love you too, Gracie."

Hurrying upstairs, she threw on jeans and a t-shirt, shoved her feet into a pair of sneakers, and quickly wrangled her wild mess of curls into a ponytail. Adding a little lip gloss, and even a touch of Laynie's mascara, she decided she wasn't going to analyze why she wanted to look pretty for him, and just leave it at the fact that she liked him.

Back downstairs, she grabbed her new cell phone, and a purse with a little cash and a credit card, and joined Matthew back on the porch. "I'm ready to go."

"I thought we could have dinner after," Matthew said as he took her hand and led her down the garden path to his car.

"So ... like a date?" The idea didn't scare her like she thought it would. "Matthew?" she prodded when he didn't answer.

"I promised you I'd take things as slow as you needed, just be your friend."

"So, not a date." There was definite disappointment there which told her everything she needed to know about these growing feelings for Matthew that she had.

"A half date. A date but not a real date. A no pressure date. Hell, Grace, I want this to be a date, but I don't want you to feel like I'm breaking my word to you." His eyes took on a tortured look as he raked his hands through his hair.

"A date," she said, reaching out to take his hands, easing them down to his sides, then touching a kiss to his cheek.

"Really?" His eyes which just moments ago had been dark and dull, now sparked with a brightness she couldn't help but feel the same spark light inside her.

"Dinner and learning to shoot? I think that's a pretty cool first date."

He returned her grin and stooped to kiss her cheek, his lips brushing the corners of her mouth. "Definitely a cool date."

The first of many she hoped.

Grace couldn't help but feel like she was rocking this rebuilding her life thing. She was looking into registering for school and she had a job lined up. After saving a bit she could find her own place, she was going to get a dog, and she was going on a date with a guy she actually cared about and could see herself falling in love with down the road.

Now all she needed was for the nightmares, the need to keep checking over her shoulder, and the guilt every time she thought of the women who weren't as lucky to survive Emmanuel's fable games to go away. The fear that lingered deep in her soul, threatening to dig its claws into her and drag her down also needed to go. But maybe if she added enough positives, they could outweigh the negatives and she could become normal again.

~

8:41 P.M.

"I didn't do very well. Again," Grace said with a sigh as she looked at the paper target.

"Hey," Matthew said, taking her shoulders and turning her to face him. "The first round of shots you fired you didn't even hit the target. The second round you only hit it once right at the very edge of the shoulder. Third round you hit it twice. Fourth round you got four. This time you hit the target with every single one of your shots. I'd say that's definite improvement."

"You hit it every single time and look how all your shots are centered right in the middle, mine are all over the place." She didn't look convinced, but in reality, she'd taken to shooting like a duck to water, that she'd managed to hit the target every time on only her fifth attempt was amazing.

"I've been doing this a whole lot longer than you have remember, honey. And honestly, you're doing great. You're hitting the target, that's the main thing. If you ever have to use a weapon to protect yourself, even if you hit your attacker in the arm or leg, you're going to slow them down, giving you a chance to get away."

The very thought of Grace having to defend herself, fight for her life once more, maybe even have to take a life—something he knew would take a terrible toll on her just as the lives of the women she'd been forced to kill weighed on her—made him feel ill. But someone couldn't be by her side twenty-four hours a day, and he knew it wasn't what she wanted anyway.

There was pride there as well though, mingled with the sick ball of fear. Grace wasn't giving up, she wasn't backing down, she was determined to rebuild her life, and he was definitely more than a little in awe of her strength.

Strength, beauty, and a big heart, he'd hit the trifecta with this woman.

"I thought it would be easier," Grace said. "It looks easy when you do it."

"You'll get better with practice."

"Can we do another round?"

"One more," he agreed. Matthew knew that if he let her, she'd stay here all night, practicing over and over again until she mastered the skill. His girl had a stubborn streak a mile wide and given that it had kept her alive for so many years as Emmanuel's prisoner, he guessed he couldn't really be unhappy about it.

He set up another paper target while Grace reloaded her weapon just as he'd taught her. He'd done the safety run through with her. Never put your finger on the trigger until you're ready to shoot, never point it at a person unless you plan on shooting them. They'd tried out a couple of guns and she seemed most comfortable with a 9mm, and once she had it ready they both put on their ear protection.

"Feet apart, shoulders relaxed, elbows locked," he coached.

Grace adjusted her position, her face the picture of concentration, the tip of her tongue poking out between her plump, pink lips, definitely the most kissable pair of lips he'd ever seen.

Then she emptied the clip into the paper target.

Given that Grace had been forced to shoot and kill before he'd worried that she'd have flashbacks, even though she'd said this was something that she wanted to do. She had been remarkably calm though, the only give away that she was thinking about what she'd been made to do was the shaking in her hands when they'd first begun the lesson. As much as he was proud of her for working so hard to get her life back, he couldn't help but feel like her holding in her emotions, trying to shove them away where they couldn't hurt her, wasn't going to end well for her.

There was only so long you could run from your emotions before they caught up with you.

He knew, he'd tried to run from his after he'd killed his stepfather and it hadn't worked.

It wouldn't work for Grace either.

"Let's see how you did," he said as he brought the paper target back in. "Wow," he said when it reached them. "Grace, you hit center mass every time but once."

Her blue eyes sparkled. "I did," she squealed.

"You did great, tonight," he told her.

"Really?"

"More than really. You're a natural. A few more lessons and you might even be able to outshoot me."

She giggled like he hoped she would. "When can we come back?"

"How about we do a lesson a week until you're comfortable, and then we'll get all your paperwork filled out and you can buy your very own gun," he suggested.

"Are you going to be my instructor for every lesson?"

"Absolutely."

"Good." The smile she gave him was shy and he knew that this whole dating thing was as weird for her as it was for him. Matthew didn't date, he'd had no plans on opening up his heart to anyone after knowing the pain of betrayal. His mother and sister cutting him out of their lives after he killed his stepfather had completely decimated his ability to trust. He'd been content to keep his friends at a distance and his interactions with women as purely a way to deal with his physical needs.

Then along came Grace with her big blue eyes, blonde curls, and intoxicating mix of vulnerability and strength, and he was a goner.

When Jem Bennett had called and asked if he'd take Grace for a shooting lesson, he'd taken advantage of the opportunity to find out a bit more of what Grace was like before her abduction. Jem had warned him that her big heart had gotten her hurt a few times when she'd seen the best in people who ended up using her. He'd learned her high school boyfriend had dumped her when they went to different colleges, and her college boyfriend had ended up cheating on her. Even if her experience with men had been amazing, after everything that had happened to her it was bound to be weird and scary putting her trust in a man.

Which was why he was determined not to do anything to make her regret the trust she was so graciously handing him.

They packed up, returned the weapons, and headed out to the parking lot. Matthew snagged her hand and was pleased when her fingers curled so naturally around his. He could get used to this, holding hands, it seemed so simple, but it was something he'd never done with a woman. All his past relationships hadn't lasted past a month, usually by then a woman started expecting a level of intimacy he hadn't been willing to give.

With Grace he wanted to give it all, everything he had.

It was the craziest thing, and he really hadn't known her long enough to be even thinking about the future, but he felt like he'd known her so much longer than a few days. No doubt because he'd spent so many hours helping the Bennetts search for her.

Not ready for the evening to end yet, he paused beside his car. "You want to grab some ice cream on the way back to your brother's place?"

"Mmm, yeah," she quickly agreed, a dreamy look on her face.

"You're adorable, you know that?" he asked with a laugh as he smoothed a lock of hair off her cheek and tucked it behind her ear.

Grace scrunched up her nose, making her look like a little rabbit. "Adorable?"

"The cutest."

"Is that how you see me? Just as someone who's cute?"

The doubt in her eyes told him that she was still struggling to make sense of who she was now and how she fitted into the world. Taking her face between his hands he met her gaze and held it so there could be no doubt about what he was about to say. "I think you are the most beautiful woman I've ever set eyes on. You're gorgeous, and when I'm with you it takes every ounce of my self-control not to ravish every inch of your stunning body. This is what you do to me, sweetheart." Grasping her wrist, he moved one of her hands to brush between his legs where he had been fighting against his body's reaction to her all night. Not an easy thing to do when she stood there like a warrior learning to shoot a gun. "I want you so bad I know I'm going to dream about you tonight. But I respect you, and I know you're still trying to get your feet beneath you, so I'm not going to do anything about it yet. Doesn't mean I don't want to though, honey. Doesn't mean I won't do something about it when the time is right. When you're ready."

Grace was staring up at him, eyes wide, breathing ragged, just as his own was. "You're almost too good to be true."

He smiled wildly and leaned down to kiss her forehead. "Not too good to be true, just a man who knows something worth waiting for when he sees it."

～

10:09 P.M.

"That was the best ice cream I've ever had," Grace said as she finished off the last spoonful. She'd made it last as long as she could while she and Matthew had strolled through the park and then driven back to Jem and Laynie's place.

Okay, it wasn't really the ice cream she was trying to make last.

It was the date.

They'd had Chinese food on the way to the range, and it was clear Matthew had asked about her favorites because he knew exactly what to order. Even when she'd gotten a little frustrated with herself that her shooting wasn't as good as his—even though she'd known there was no way she could outshoot a cop her first try—he'd been calm and patient, and she'd had a lot of fun.

All those memories of the women she'd been forced to kill that she had been so afraid would take over had been there, but Matthew's presence had kept them at bay, and she'd been able to focus on what she was doing. One thing was for sure, Grace was never going to be anyone's prisoner again. Not Emmanuel and not any of the other sick monsters roaming the earth.

"Couldn't agree more," Matthew said as he pulled into the driveway. "Although I think it has more to do with the company than the actual ice cream."

"Couldn't agree more," she echoed. As much as she loved a good hot fudge sundae topped with nuts, sprinkles, chocolate chips, and the traditional cherry on top, it was absolutely the company that made this one her favorite. She got along so well with Matthew. They talked, he made her laugh, he hadn't held back about his dark past which meant she hadn't felt the need to hold back about her abduction. They just ... clicked.

"I'll walk you to the door." He unbuckled his seatbelt, but she reached out to stop him.

"It's okay, you don't need to, it's literally about fifteen steps to the porch." The last thing she needed in her life was another overprotective big brother. She had two already, plus her sisters-in-law and she didn't want another. While she understood Matthew wasn't just a cop but the one who rescued her and was working her case, she wanted to be more than that to him. Never once tonight had he made her feel like a victim, until now.

"Hey," he said soothingly, capturing her hand and cradling it in his much larger one. "I didn't mean to upset you, I'm sorry."

Grace huffed out a breath. She was being overly sensitive, projecting her own worries onto Matthew. She was the one who was worried about forever being the victim, she didn't want this one thing to define her. It was probably why she was so driven to rebuild her life, she wanted to be more than just a kidnap victim. "No, I'm the one who should be sorry, I snapped at you because of my own insecurities. I want to be more than just Emmanuel's victim. My brothers and their wives hover and fuss, and I know they love me, and I know they suffered too, but I want you to see me. The real me. I'm still in here. Different than the Grace I was before but still me. That's the person I want you to see when you look at me, not someone who has to be walked to her door because she can't do it on her own."

"Sweetheart," he said softly and reached out to feather his fingertips across her temple. "I wanted to walk you to the door because it's what a gentleman does after a date, and because I want to wring out every last second of time I get to spend with you."

"Oh," the word fluttered from her lips on a breath of air as she saw the fiery heat in his eyes. Was he going to kiss her goodnight? "Now I feel stupid for jumping to conclusions."

Matthew laughed and the tension eased. "Come on."

While she unbuckled, Matthew rounded the car and opened her door for her, taking her hand as she stood up. They walked in silence up the porch steps and then stood there staring at one another.

Grace felt suddenly awkward and unsure. She wanted him to kiss her, but she wasn't sure how to ask him to. He'd told her that he saw her as more than just a victim, and he'd given her no reason to doubt that, and yet still this felt different than the end to other dates she'd had. Then she'd always known it would end in a kiss at the door, or after they'd been dating a while taking things inside, but with Matthew she had that nervous swirly feeling in her stomach. No butterflies for her, more like stampeding t-rexes.

Their eyes met.

Metaphorical sparks arced between them.

When Matthew curled a hand around the back of her neck she didn't pull away.

When his other hand curled around her waist, settling on her hip, she moved in closer.

Her head tiled up, his tilted down.

The dinosaurs stomping in her belly faded, replaced with a raw need she'd never felt before.

Grace had lost her virginity to her high school boyfriend in their junior year. She'd slept with her college boyfriend, sex had always been nice, something she'd enjoyed, and her college boyfriend had been good at it, known how to work her body, but neither of her lovers had made her feel like this.

And Matthew hadn't even kissed her yet.

His lips brushed across hers and a sigh rumbled through his body, and then he was kissing her properly. His tongue prodded at her lips, and when she opened it swept inside her mouth, he devoured her, possessed her. Between them she could feel his length hardening and she shifted uncomfortably as a throbbing between her legs made her hot and needy.

She wanted this.

Wanted more.

Wanted it all.

It felt impossible that this time last week she was still locked in

Emmanuel's house, being punished for some perceived wrongdoing. Just days had passed since she had been rescued, but somehow it felt like she had lived an entire lifetime in those few days.

"Are you done mauling my baby sister on my front porch?"

The angry voice had Matthew stepping back and they both turned to see Jem glaring at them. Laynie was standing behind her husband with a more sympathetic expression on her face, and yet she didn't tell Jem to back off.

"What do you think you're doing?" she demanded. "You're the one who set this up, asked Matthew to give me a shooting lesson, and told him my favorite Chinese foods. You knew this was a date. How did you think it was going to end?"

"Not with him mauling you like that," Jem muttered.

"Look, Jem, I know you don't want to hear this, but I'm not the same naïve girl I used to be. I'm stronger now, tougher, I had to be if I wanted to live. And I *do* want to live. I want to be a real person again, not Emmanuel's toy, and not your sweet baby sister. I want to be me. The new me. I want to build a new life, and I want that life to include Matthew. I love you so much, both of you," she added to include Laynie. "Elijah and Ali too. I love you more than you can ever know, and I appreciate you all so much. I'm so grateful that you're letting me stay here, that you're supporting me going back to school and getting a job, even though I know you want to keep me close. But you need to accept that I can take care of myself. I've been doing just that for five and a half years. As much as I love you, I cannot allow anyone to ever again dictate to me what I can and can't do. So, if I want to kiss Matthew goodnight after the best date I've ever had, then I'm going to do it. I like him. A lot." She turned slightly so she could see Matthew and her cheeks pinked when she saw the pride shining from his eyes. "He understands me, he makes me feel normal, and even if things between us don't work out, I know he'll be my friend forever. I need to be in control of my own life, so don't ever come and interrupt a kiss I wanted to happen again. Goodnight, Matthew, thank you for tonight it was perfect. Almost." She shot her big brother a reproving frown, then stood on tiptoe to kiss Matthew's cheek.

"Night, Grace, sweet dreams," Matthew said as she ducked past her brother and into the house.

Tonight had been everything she'd hoped it would be and so much more. Even her brother's interruption couldn't dampen the hope soaring within her. A normal life was within her grasp, and she had Matthew to thank for that. Everything she'd done to survive was finally paying off. She was free and she was ... happy.

CHAPTER *Six*

July 11th
8:57 A.M.

"All right, let's get things started, we have a lot to get through," Heidi announced.

At his boss' words the room fell silent, all eyes turning to look at her. Matthew had hardly been able to get the smile off his face since he'd said goodnight to Grace last night. Not only had their date been a blast, but watching her put her brother in his place had been nothing short of awe inspiring. Like Grace, he understood where the Bennett family was coming from, but seeing Grace exert her independence, take control of her life, made him so very proud of her. If ever there was a victim who stood a great chance at rebuilding their life, it was Grace.

Of course, he knew better than most the scars left behind. But Grace was the definition of a survivor, and he would be right there beside her, offering her his support whenever she needed it.

"Kane, any hits yet?" Heidi asked the crime scene tech.

"No, I would have called you all immediately if I got anything. I think we have to accept that Emmanuel isn't in any databases," Kane replied, shooting an apologetic glance Allina's way. Grace's sister-in-law had joined them today and while Matthew didn't think that was a good idea, Ali was way too personally invested to be objective, it wasn't his place to decide who was in and out of the meeting. Besides, he'd been worried if he pushed too hard then he'd wind up getting himself kicked off the case. It wasn't like he was a whole lot less emotionally invested in Grace's wellbeing than Ali was.

Bringing Grace closure had become as important to him as learning about her and being there for her. In Grace his mind seemed to see a second chance, a chance to save someone this time who wanted to be saved. His mother and sister had blamed him for what he'd done, painted him as the villain in the story even though he was only an eleven-year-old boy. Maybe this time he wanted to be the hero.

Grace's hero.

"How can he not have a criminal record?" Heidi demanded to no one in particular.

"Something triggered him," Matthew replied.

"Still to go straight to kidnapping and murder without any other stops along the way isn't what we usually see," Heidi said.

"But he didn't kill any of the victims directly, except Mable White," Rylla reminded her. "And he sees himself as some sort of God. Emmanuel isn't his real name, he chose it for a reason, testing these women and teaching them lessons that mean something only to him. He let the women die as a result of his games, in his mind that's not killing him. My guess would be that Natalie Potter was his first violent kill. Not that he's not absolutely and completely one hundred percent responsible for every one of his victims' deaths."

Matthew agreed with his partner's assessment, especially since he knew Emmanuel had forced Grace to shoot the women who lost their test but didn't die as a result of it. It seemed Emmanuel hadn't been comfortable being hands on with the killing. While he'd told Rylla about Grace's admission—only after letting Grace know he had to tell his partner—he didn't know if Grace had told her family yet, and didn't want to spill her secrets in front of her sister-in-law if she wasn't ready for them to know.

"Then how are we going to find him?" Heidi asked in frustration.

"Rylla and I were able to link some of the victims together but none of them can be linked to one location," Matthew explained. "So, we started looking at Natalie's death. Since we believe she was killed in frustration after Emmanuel's attempts at getting Grace back failed, we assumed that he wouldn't have had time to find her and therefore he already knew her."

Heidi's eyes lit up. "So, we need to look into Natalie's life, find someone in her circle who could fit the profile of our kidnapper."

Matthew nodded. "Rylla and I have been doing that, but there are a lot of people, and we haven't found anyone yet who we think could be Emmanuel."

Rylla glanced hesitantly at him and then over at Ali, who had been sitting quietly beside her partner Jonathon, listening but so far not saying anything. Then his partner dragged in a deep breath and announced to the room. "I do have one idea on how we can find Emmanuel."

No one said anything for a moment, but Matthew knew just from the look on Rylla's face that he wasn't going to like her plan. From the looks on Ali and Jonathon's faces they felt the same way.

"Well?" Heidi prompted.

"Well," Rylla started slowly, "we know that Emmanuel is fixated on Grace. He's made his intentions clear, he's not going to stop making attempts at getting her back." She held up a hand when Ali opened her mouth to speak, halting the other woman. "We can use that to our advantage."

Matthew's body had a visceral reaction to the very idea of putting Grace in danger like that. "Bait," he choked out. "You want to use her as bait?"

"Absolutely not," Ali said, almost springing out of her chair. Jonathon's hand on her shoulder was the only thing that stopped her.

"Ali," Heidi started.

"No," Ali cut off their boss. Even though they weren't biologically related, Grace looked a lot like her sister-in-law. They were both petite, both had wild blonde curls, and blue eyes. Both were fierce and determined, and both were stronger than they looked if you were only looking at the packaging and not what was inside. "Grace is barely holding it together, she seems strong and tough, and I'm not saying she's not, but inside she's vulnerable and fragile, and she's not really dealing with anything she's just pretending it never happened. She has no training and isn't equipped for what you're suggesting."

Righteous anger wiped away some of the fear. "You're not giving her the credit she deserves," he told Ali. "Look at everything she survived without any so-called training. Yes, she is avoiding for now, but she's doing it for a reason. To feel safe, to begin moving on, she has to feel like she's in control of her actions, that's why she's focused right now on her future not the past. Does she need to deal with it, absolutely, and she will when she's ready. The idea of using Grace as bait makes me feel sick, but I believe that she'll want to do it."

"Grace is vulnerable right now, we won't allow her to be used," Ali said, fire practically shooting from her eyes.

"She'll want to do it. You know I'm right. And if you try to pull rank and stop her from doing it, she's going to feel like you're no better than Emmanuel." At the hurt that flashed across Ali's face he softened his tone. "You know I'm right, Ali. She knows you love her, but she's made it clear what she needs right now is freedom, autonomy. After so long being kept prisoner, she needs to be in control of her own life. She'll want to do this," he said again.

Defeated, Ali sighed and nodded. "I don't like it, but unfortunately, I think you're right. What did you have in mind, Rylla."

"Trust me, I know what I'm asking of your whole family. I know how terrified I was when my sister was taken, but I believe this will be the safest option for Grace," Rylla said. "I was thinking we move her to a safe house, play that up, allow it to leak to the media. We'll have someone stay in the house with her and then a couple of cops watching the house. Then all we have to do it wait for Emmanuel to turn up and arrest him. End of story, Grace will be safe, won't have to be constantly looking over her shoulder, and all those other families will get closure."

As much as he hated this idea, Matthew also knew it held merit. Emmanuel wouldn't stop to wonder why a safehouse location had been leaked, he would be too focused on his chance to get to Grace. There was no way he would be able to pass up an opportunity to get to her.

No way.

Just like there was no way he wasn't going to be the cop staying with Grace in the house. He didn't care who was watching over them from outside, but he needed to be there with Grace. She'd say yes to this in a heartbeat, she'd want to do it as penance for being forced to kill some of Emmanuel's victims, but that didn't mean it wouldn't be hard for her. Being stuck in a house was bound to give her flashbacks and having to put her moving forward plan on hold would force her to confront the memories and emotions she was running from.

She'd need him, and he needed to be there for her.

~

12:24 P.M.

They were really doing this.

Grace looked at the nondescript house whose driveway they had just pulled into and tried to calm her racing heart.

Of course, she had agreed to the plan for her to play bait as soon as it was presented to her. What else could she do? While she understood in a logical sense that she had been forced to point a gun at those women and shoot them, she'd had zero other options other than be killed herself, guilt over taking their lives would be something she would carry around with her for the rest of her life.

Perhaps playing a role in seeing the man responsible brought to justice could ease a little of that weight. Adjust the scales a little in her favor. Even if it didn't, this was something she had to do. For them and for her.

For so long she hadn't had any power where Emmanuel was concerned. She was his helpless prisoner, forced to play a role in his games against her will, punished for every perceived infraction. This time she wanted to be the one with the power. The one to take away his free will by having him thrown in prison.

If this worked.

"Are you sure he's not going to think it's weird that the location of a safehouse was leaked?" she asked. Even though they'd gone over every-thing at the station before she and Matthew packed bags and drove here, she still had questions about the validity of the plan.

"We believe he's going to be too focused on a chance to get to you to even consider anything else," Matthew replied. He didn't seem bothered by having to repeat answers to questions she'd already asked, and his calming presence did help to slow her heart rate down a little.

"Isn't allowing a safehouse's location to leak dangerous? What happens to the next person who needs to stay here?" The last thing Grace needed were any more deaths on her conscience. And if the fact that the safehouse's location was no longer safe led to someone else's death, she would blame herself.

"It's not a real safehouse," Matthew told her. "It's just a house that belongs to another detective in homicide. He's moving, he and his family already bought another house, and this one was on the market. After we use it, we'll make sure it's well publicized that the house has been sold, so no one would ever have a reason to come looking for anyone in police protective custody here."

His words reassured her a little, and they both climbed out of the car. The house was a brick two-story with a simple front yard, just grass and one large tree. Four windows gazed out of the house's front, two on the first floor and two on the second. Despite looking like basically every other house on the block it had a nice homey feel about it. She could see a family living here, bikes lying on the grass, maybe a swing hanging from one of the tree's branches.

If she was going to get married and have kids, this was exactly the kind of home she would want to raise her family in.

Of course, her gaze immediately went to Matthew at the thought of marriage and children. Despite her family's objections, he had been adamant that he be the one to stay here with her and she was glad. He was the one she wanted by her side as they played a dangerous game with a dangerous killer. Her family would be able to keep her safe, she had no doubt about that, but the chance to spend quality one on one time with the man she couldn't stop thinking about was something she couldn't resist.

He grabbed both their suitcases, then took her hand with his spare one. It all felt so natural that it was almost hard for her to keep the reason they were here at the front of her mind. That was something she was going to have to work on. While she knew Matthew was also glad to have this time to get to know each other better this was also work for him. His job was to protect her, and she knew he took that seriously, so she was going to have to work on not being too big a distraction.

Together, they crossed the yard and the small porch, and Matthew unlocked the front door and ushered her inside. The house had one large room with two doors on the back wall. The kitchen was to their left, a couple of sofas and a TV to their right, and in between the two spaces was a large wooden dining table. The homey feel continued inside, the walls were a warm cream, the floor was wooden floorboards, the kitchen cabinets were the same color wood as the floor, and the two big, brown leather couches all but screamed come and curl up on me.

"The door on the left is the laundry room and downstairs powder room, there's also a door leading out to the backyard," Matthew told her. "The other door leads to a media room. Upstairs there are three bedrooms, you can take the master which has its own bathroom, and I can take one of the other bedrooms."

Disappointment at the thought of them not sharing a room surprised her.

Was she ready to share a bed with a man?

She hadn't been with one in a really long time and her last sexual experience had been ... nope, not going there today. That was just another in a long line of things she was going to have to process and deal with but not today.

Today had enough worries of its own.

"There's also a really cool firepit in the backyard and a pool, so if you didn't pack a bathing suit, we'll have to get you one because we have to take a swim later."

Grace laughed. "I packed one, you told me about the pool almost as soon as I agreed to play bait. Then you told me again when we went by Jem and Laynie's house so I could pack. Then you told me *again* in the car on the way here."

Matthew laughed along with her. "Swimming is one of my favorite things to do. Plus, I'm not going to pass up an opportunity to see you in a bikini."

The heat in his eyes had her body immediately responding, her breasts seemed to grow heavier, an ache formed between her legs, her skin felt extra sensitive beneath the sundress she was wearing. "What makes you think I packed a bikini?" she asked breathily.

"Wishful thinking." He set both suitcases down and took a deliberate step toward her.

She didn't back up, and when his hands rested on her bare shoulders, trailing down to her wrists and back up again her skin broke out into a mass of tingly goosebumps. "I packed a bikini. It's blue."

"To match your eyes."

Grace nodded, currently unable to form words. How was she supposed to think of anything but the weight of Matthew's large hands on her shoulders. Hands she knew would never be used against her to inflict pain. But what kind of pleasure could they give?

She wanted to find out.

Angling her body closer so it was flush against Matthew's, she tilted her head up, watched as his eyes flared with desire and his head tipped down. Anticipation was a sweet kind of torture. His warm breath caressed her skin a second before his lips claimed hers.

Fiery desire scorched along every one of her nerves, and her hands curled around his hips, drawing him closer.

After everything she had been through, she had never thought she could feel this good, this alive, this free.

A rap on the door had them both reluctantly pulling back.

"That will be the cops who'll be watching the house," Matthew told her. "They're dropping off some groceries and checking in, so why don't you go and unpack, get settled, and then we'll have some lunch. After that we're going for a swim, and, Grace, I can't wait to see you in that bikini."

A pleasant flush warmed her cheeks, and she couldn't help but picture how ridiculously sexy Matthew was going to look in his own bathing suit. Taking her suitcase, she hurried up the stairs, still surprised it was possible for her to feel this comfortable and secure around a man. Matthew had taken her completely by surprise, and her growing feelings for him were the last thing she expected to have right now, but there were still things about her he didn't know.

Not things to do with Emmanuel, but from before.

She had to tell him, she knew that. It was the right thing to do, really the *only* thing to do, and yet she couldn't quite squash the worry that it would change things.

So far, Matthew had been understanding about everything, and it hadn't seemed to affect the way he saw her, but this was different. This couldn't help but make things different.

~

5:46 P.M.

He could stare at her forever.

In fact, Matthew had to keep reminding himself that as much as he was looking forward to spending this time with Grace, he was here to protect her.

Maybe if he kept repeating that he'd stop getting distracted by those long limbs and soft curves.

It was obvious that Grace hadn't been outside in years. Her skin was as white as snow, and she'd been diligently reapplying sunblock every hour, so she didn't wind up with horrible sunburn. Even though she was short, only five-foot-three, her legs were long and slim, and the small curve of her hips had him wanting to dig his fingers into them as he thrust into her until both their worlds exploded into pleasure. Her breasts weren't large, but they were the perfect size to fit into his hands and all he could think about was how sensitive her nipples would be when he finally got his hands—and his mouth—on them.

When, not if, because he could feel the sexual tension building between them.

Not that he would do anything until Grace was ready. This was her show, and she would have to be the one to let him know when she was ready for more.

Grace stretched, the movement sending a jolt of blood straight to his groin and he shifted uncomfortably. He was sitting on the edge of the pool with his legs dangling in the water. Grace was lying on a towel on the tiles around the pool, soaking up the sun's rays.

"Matthew?" she asked as she sat up slowly, blinking in the bright sunlight.

"Right here."

"My stomach is rumbling so loud it woke me up. You want to go inside and have dinner?"

"Sure thing, sweetheart."

She paused in the act of standing up and shot him a sweet smile. "I like when you call me sweetheart. I never thought I would be affected by pet names like that, terms of endearments, but every time you say that I get this tingly feeling in my stomach."

Matthew dove into the water, swam across the pool, and climbed out on the other side. He stalked toward her like a predator stalking its prey only this prey very obviously wanted to be caught if the fluttering of her pulse and fire in her eyes were anything to go by. When he reached her, he yanked her up against him, no soft and sweet this time, he plundered her mouth in a scorching kiss that put the summer sun to shame.

"Come on, sweetheart, let's go do dinner," he said when he was able to drag himself away from her. Matthew managed it only because he knew if he didn't stop there, he wouldn't be able to stop at all.

Hand in hand, they headed back inside. After spending the afternoon outside it seemed overly dark inside, but they still had several hours yet before the sun would set. Once it did, he would be on high alert as he doubted Emmanuel would try anything until he could use the cover of darkness. For now, he was just going to soak up every second of time he got to spend with Grace, falling for her further with each new thing he learned about her.

"What do you want to eat?" he asked. They had a well-stocked fridge and cupboards, so they could pretty much make whatever they wanted.

"I'm not in the mood to cook much. We could make a pasta salad?" she suggested. "That was my favorite summer dinner when I was growing up. Oh, and while we leave it in the fridge to cool down, we could make meringues for dessert."

"I thought we'd make S'mores and sit by the firepit later."

Grace made a face. "I don't like S'mores, marshmallows are icky."

"Icky, huh?" he asked with a smirk.

"Totally. I always just used to eat the cookies when we make S'mores, and the chocolate of course. But meringues, they're delicious, and we only need eggs, sugar, and a little vanilla. Ooh, and if we have food coloring, we can make multi-colored meringues! I'd been wanting to make some with more than one color but then Emmanuel and ... well you know what happened there."

"Okay, pasta salad and meringues it is."

"What do we have in the fridge?" Grace opened the fridge door and answered her own question. "Tomatoes, cucumber, you want an onion in there?"

"Sure." Matthew grabbed a pot and filled it with water, turning on the gas and leaving it to start boiling while he found a bag of pasta in the cupboard. While he got that cooking, Grace started chopping the vegetables. Or was it fruits? Matthew always got confused with toma-toes and cucumbers. Were they fruits? Vegetables? Did it matter? Abso-lutely not. "I've never made meringues before. How do we make them?"

"They're really easy. A few eggs, we only need the whites not the yolks, a little cream of tartar, beat them until soft peaks. Then add the sugar a bit at a time, beating until its stiff and glossy. Then beat in the vanilla, and color if we have any. Then we put them in the oven and cook them until they're hard on the outside, not sticky. Usually I can tell because you can move them without them sticking to the paper."

He stared at her with his mouth hanging open. "You may as well have just spoken a different language."

"I thought you said you liked to cook."

"Cook, not bake," he corrected.

Grace giggled. "It's all the same. And it's easy, really. Once we get the salad in the fridge, I'll show you."

They worked side by side. Grace did the chopping, he watched the pasta. Once it was cooked, he drained it, ran it under cool water to take some of the heat out, then put it in a bowl. Grace added the vegetables

—or fruits—and a little dressing, once it was all mixed together, they set it in the fridge.

"How many eggs?" he asked.

"Three, but before we crack them, we better check to see if we have cream of tartar. It's not the kind of thing your friends might have thought to stock."

"I don't think that's going to be a problem, honey." Now that he knew how much she liked it when he used terms of endearments, he'd be using them as often as he could. And she also liked pet names, he'd have to come up with one for her.

"Why not?"

"Your brothers gave a list of your favorite foods so I'm pretty sure that if they knew you liked to bake meringues then whatever ingredients you needed would have been on the list." He went to the cupboard, searched through the pantry, quickly locating the cream of tartar. "Here you go, curly."

She froze, her hand partially outstretched. "Curly?"

Matthew shrugged and then winked. "You said you liked pet names."

"You couldn't come up with one that made me sound older than six?"

From the smile curving up her lips, he knew she actually liked the nickname. "Well, you are adorable." He paused to kiss her forehead on his way to the fridge. Then whispered in her ear, "And the most gorgeous woman I've ever seen."

When he turned from the fridge, eggs in hand, he was pleased to see her cheeks stained with the prettiest shade of pink. She really was the most amazing woman, so many different sides to her, such strength, such beauty, she was an absolute delight, and he loved every taste he'd gotten of her. Could even imagine wanting to touch her, taste her, make her smile every day for the rest of his life.

"All right, you're the boss here, curly. Tell me what to do."

Grace hesitated. "If you don't want to bake, we don't have to. I can just eat cookies tonight when you make your S'mores."

"Sweetheart, if I haven't already made it clear I don't care what we do as long as we're spending time together, then let me assure you that's exactly how I feel. I wish it wasn't like this, that you weren't in danger and playing bait because that makes me sick to my stomach. But this," he waved a hand between them, "is real. This is fun for me, and I'm going to enjoy your company."

She offered up a shy smile. "I like being here with you too. It would be nice if we weren't waiting for a killer to come after me. But being here with you is fun."

"Then let's get baking your meringues. Oh, and, curly, I saw food coloring in the pantry, so we can do colored meringues."

"Oh, yay." She clapped her hands in delight. "Do they have all the colors? Let's make unicorn ones, pink, yellow, and purple I think. Those colors should go well together, and I've never tried more than two together before so I probably shouldn't try more than three this time around."

Matthew just stared at her, transfixed by the smile on her lips.

Such a genuine smile.

It was easy to see that it reached down to her soul and uncurled out to every part of her being.

That she could still find joy in the small things in life was inspiring, and Matthew wished that he'd been able to work through and move forward from what had happened to him as a kid as well as Grace was forging a new path. Already Grace had taught him the importance of seeking peace and focusing on the future. He was lucky to have her here, and even luckier that she wanted him as much as he wanted her.

CHAPTER
Seven

July 12th
3:31 A.M.

"Hold her down."

Grace tried to fight the pair of hands that circled her wrists and kick at the hands trying to grab her ankles, but her body wouldn't co-operate properly.

What was wrong with her?

"Look at her try to fight," a voice sneered, and she looked into a pair of eyes she had trusted.

How could she have been so stupid?

She knew better.

Knew better than to come to a party alone where the only one she knew was a man who was supposed to be a friend.

Knew better than to take a drink offered to her when she had no way to know what was in it.

Knew better than to wander off by herself in an attempt to leave rather than immediately grab her phone and call one of her brothers when she realized she was in trouble.

Now she was going to pay the price.

"She's hot," another voice said, and even in her drugged state she could hear the heavy weight of lust.

"Back off, she's mine. I went to enough trouble to get her here since she wouldn't put out. No one touches her but me."

How did she not see who he really was?

She'd thought he was a friend, she'd trusted him. They'd studied together, and while, yes, she had resisted his advances, making it clear she wasn't ready for another relationship so soon after her ex cheated on her, she'd thought he understood.

Her pants were undone and shoved down her legs enough to bare her panties which were ripped off her body and tossed aside. Tears leaked from her eyes as her drugged body tried fruitlessly to fight the man who settled between her spread legs and his friends who held her down ...

"Fight, Grace. If you want to live you have to fight."

The sudden appearance of Emmanuel standing above her startled her.

What was he doing there?

He hadn't been there that night.

Then she noticed the metal cuff circling her neck, chaining her to the floor. There were cuffs around her ankles, and one around her hips as well. Rendering her helpless.

A blade glinted above her, and she realized she was holding onto the knife handle. It was attached to something, a spring of some sort, and she knew if she let go it would send the blade piercing through her chest.

Her arms shook.

She couldn't do this.

"Remember the story of the crow and the pitcher," Emmanuel said, glancing between her and something off to the side.

Grace turned her head.

Saw another woman there, bound with a knife above her, just as she was.

"Persistence," Emmanuel continued, "there is always a way, never give up. If you want to live you have to keep trying. Your life is in your own hands."

She could do this.

Sooner or later her arms would give out.

It wasn't a matter of persistence it was simply a fact.

Eventually her arms would give out and the knife would pierce her heart, killing her ...

"Shoot her," Emmanuel ordered.

"No." *Grace shook her head wildly. Why was he asking her to kill the woman? So she had lost the fable game. If Emmanuel hadn't set the game up to kill the loser and wanted the woman dead then why didn't he kill her himself?*

"She failed, she dies," *Emmanuel said, his eyes cold like he had no soul.* "Kill her."

"I can't," *Grace sobbed.*

"Then I will kill you."

"No, please, don't make me." *She had fought so long to stay alive, to win his games, to survive, but she couldn't take another woman's life. Especially not one who had fallen victim to the same monster she had.*

"Kill her," *Emmanuel screamed.*

She should kill him.

But if she did that, she was signing her own death warrant. The metal cuff around her ankle was attached to a chain that was attached to a metal hook embedded in the concrete floor. She had no way out unless Emmanuel got the key from the other room and let her go. If she killed him, she killed herself and the other woman anyway.

"Kill her, do it now, or I'll kill you. Do it, kill her. Kill her!"

Sobbing, Grace closed her eyes, unable to look at the woman she was about to murder. She pressed the barrel of the gun against the woman's head and pulled the trigger. She was crying so hard she felt like she was going to shatter into a million pieces.

What had she done?

"Grace!"

"Grace!"

"Grace, wake up. Now."

The voice was commanding. It allowed no room for anything other than obedience, and somehow, her body managed to yank itself from the dream.

Blinking open heavy eyes, Grace found herself tangled in the sheets. She was on her knees, Matthew was in front of her on the mattress, also on his knees, his hands gripping her shoulders with a near bruising force.

"You back with me?" he asked, smoothing away a curl that was stuck to her wet cheek.

"Yeah," she assured him in a shaky voice, wanting to wipe away the worry in his eyes. But really that was a lie. How could she ever be okay again after the things she had done? It had been a long time since she'd dreamed about her rape, it was just a couple of months later that she'd been abducted and by then she had other things to worry about, like fighting to stay alive.

Why had she dreamed about it tonight?

Was it because of how her body responded to Matthew's? Because her subconscious knew it wasn't a matter of if, only of when that the two of them made love?

Or was it her mind trying to tell her something she didn't know she knew?

Why had the dream of her rape been followed by one of Emmanuel and his sick games and determination to control her?

It definitely wasn't uncommon for her to dream about the sick, twisted games he'd forced her to play. Or even of him making her kill those other women. But why had she dreamed about all of it tonight?

There was something she was missing, but she couldn't put her finger on what it was. It was something important thought, maybe even the key to finding Emmanuel, so she had to figure out what she didn't know that she knew.

"You're shaking." Matthew touched the back of his hand to her forehead. "And freezing. Come here, sweetheart."

Snagging the blanket, she'd shoved aside when she'd gone to bed because she was too hot—because of the warm night and her body's physical attraction to Matthew and burning need for his touch—and wrapped it around her. Then he scooped her into his arms and carried her over to the armchair in the corner of the room by the window.

"Can you open the window?" she asked after he'd sat and settled her on his lap.

"It's cooled down outside and you're already cold."

"Please, Matthew, I just need the fresh air. I feel like I'm suffocating," she admitted, a slight whimper escaping despite her efforts to hold it in.

"All right, baby." Balancing her on one knee, he leaned over and shoved the window open then curled his arms around her and snuggled her close against his chest.

As the soft breeze washed over her, Grace felt herself begin to calm, the fear and horror of the nightmare fading. Helping bring Emmanuel down wasn't enough, there weren't enough good deeds in the world for her to make up for the deeds she regretted with every fiber of her being.

"Do you want to talk about it?" Matthew's fingers combed soothingly through her tangle of curls, caressing her head with each sweep of his hand.

Grace nestled her face against his neck, breathing in the slightly woodsy scent she had come to associate with Matthew. "I feel like there's something important I don't remember. Something that will tell you who Emmanuel is."

"You'll remember." He said it so confidently that it was hard not to believe him.

Hard but not impossible.

"What if I don't?"

"Then we'll catch him when he comes here to get you, just like we planned."

"And if he doesn't?"

"Then we'll work out another plan. I promise you, Grace, we *will* find Emmanuel, and he *will* be punished for every horrible thing he did to you and all those other women."

Tilting her head back, she looked up at him, studied his strong jaw, his kind eyes, allowed his strength to become her own. "Why do you think he did it?"

"I don't know, honey. I hope that when we find him, we get the chance to ask him, but in the end it won't change anything. He did what he did and knowing why won't undo anything, it won't erase the pain he caused you." His lips brushed across her forehead. "I wish I could take that pain away from you, curly."

She smiled at the cutesy nickname, and the horror of her dreams receded a little further. "You are. I don't know how you're doing it, but somehow, you're making that pain fade little by little."

2:45 P.M.

"Come on, let's go out," Matthew announced. He couldn't take the look in Grace's eyes any longer.

She'd been different since her nightmares last night.

It was a subtle difference. If you didn't know what to look for she'd look like any other young woman enjoying lounging by the pool on a lazy summer's day. But he did know what to look for, and every time he saw the shadows lurking in her eyes it drove him crazy.

He wanted to chase those shadows away so badly, but he didn't know how to do it.

Grace was pushing herself too hard, trying to remember whatever her subconscious was attempting to tell her. There was more to her dreams than she'd been willing to share, and while he didn't doubt that if she knew something important about Emmanuel she would have shared it with him and the team, he wanted her to tell him everything because she trusted him.

Trust was a hard thing to earn. He knew this because he could count pretty much on the fingers of one hand those he trusted. His partner Rylla, her husband Nate, his boss Heidi, a few of the other cops he worked with and that was it. When your trust in others had been decimated by the very people who were supposed to love you unconditionally, it was hard to get past that.

Grace was worth the risk of getting hurt.

Matthew was under no illusions that while he was developing real feelings for the pretty curly haired blonde, her feelings might be less than genuine. Not that he thought she would do it on purpose to hurt him, but he had been the one to save her, they'd connected over the fact they had both taken lives, and she needed him to be safe.

While he wanted to believe that they might just get the happy ever after he was pretty certain neither of them quite felt they deserved, he had to be prepared for that not to happen. For Grace to realize once she started rebuilding her life, gotten her feet back beneath her, that she didn't need him after all, and that the feelings she thought she had were nothing more than gratefulness and friendship, would destroy him. After that there would never be another woman he'd allow himself to get close to.

Still, he'd settle for being Grace's friend if it was the only way to stay in her life.

Yep, he was that much of a sucker for this gorgeous woman.

"Matthew."

"Yeah?"

A small smile quirked one side of her mouth. "You keep accusing me of being distracted today and yet you were completely zoned out then."

"Sorry, sweetheart. What were you saying?"

"*You* were saying you wanted to go out, I said we've spent all day outdoors by the pool."

"No, I meant *out* out. Like, leave the property kind of out."

"Oh, are we allowed?"

"Normally if you were in protective custody then no you can't go out, but nothing about your situation is normal. We want Emmanuel to come looking for you, and we couldn't be so forthright as to completely leak the address of the safehouse, just a few photos of you being brought here. So, let's go and give things a little nudge. We'll go out for a jog, maybe head down to the little shopping mall a few streets over, we can grab a coffee, something for dinner, and maybe some more eggs so we can make more meringues."

Grace laughed at that. "We wouldn't need to make more meringues if you weren't eating five and six at a time, and then sneaking more when you think I'm not looking."

"You were right, they're delicious, and addictive. So let's make more, we can try for four colors this time," he added, trying to sweeten the deal.

"Okay, we can go out. But do we have to go jogging? I hate running, it's so awful."

"It's a great way to keep in shape." He'd been a runner since middle school. While he could get up a pretty good speed if he had to, he was more of a distance runner, he could go for miles and had competed in a few marathons over the years. "Nothing feels better than when you push past the pain and get into that zone, then you can go on forever."

Grace looked at him like he was crazy, and she looked so sweet and sexy in the blue bikini, lying on the hot pink towel, that he couldn't resist touching her. Reaching out he snagged a hold on her wrist and tugged her over to his towel, where he proceeded to tickle her.

She squealed with laughter and tried to bat away his hands. "Matthew, stop! You'll never convince me running is anything other than torture."

"Never, huh?" He kept tickling her and rolled her so she was beneath him, his knees straddling her hips, and all of a sudden he realized this was a bad idea. The playfulness morphed into something sensual, and before he even realized it, his fingers were no longer tickling Grace's stomach and sides, now they were caressing her petal soft skin.

Desire was evident in her eyes, it burned like a blue flame, and she made no move to stop him, but intuition warned him that she wasn't ready yet. So even though his body begged for just a little taste of the stunning woman lying beneath him, he knew he had to be sane enough for both of them right now. The last thing he wanted was to take things further than Grace was ready for and have her regret it. While she was still insistent that Emmanuel hadn't raped her, he couldn't get rid of the feeling that she was hiding something big from him. Something he needed to know before they did anything more physical than kissing.

Because he was still a guy, and he was insanely attracted to Grace Bennett, he captured her lips in a simple kiss that still managed to zing along his every nerve and settle itself deep in his soul.

Then he grabbed her hand and pulled her up with him. "Come on, curly, let's go for a jog."

She studied him curiously for a moment but then nodded. "Fine, but be prepared for me to complain the entire time."

Matthew laughed. "Thanks for the warning. Go change and I'll meet you at the front door in five minutes."

"Oh," she asked, twirling a curl around her finger, the absolute picture of delicious innocence. "You don't want me to go jogging dressed like this?"

He growled.

Yep, actually growled.

"No one gets to see this body but me."

Grace laughed.

Actually laughed at him.

In one of those kind of patronizing aren't you adorable, sort of ways. "I didn't know you had an alpha streak, you hid that well, Matthew. Don't forget I grew up with two big brothers. I know all about insanely protective men, but don't forget I don't let them make decisions for me and I won't let you. I'll show my body to anyone I want." With that, she tossed her hair over her shoulder and walked off, pausing at the back door. "And, Matthew, just so you know. I don't want any other man seeing my body. Only you."

With that, she disappeared inside leaving him staring after her, so hungry for a taste of her he could barely control himself.

But he did.

Because Grace was worth the wait.

While she changed, he quickly threw on shorts and a t-shirt, then stuffed his feet into a pair of sneakers, and texted the cops watching the house to let them know they'd be going out. There was always a chance that Emmanuel would do something crazy, like trying to abduct Grace from a busy hospital, and shoot him in the street to snatch Grace. She was what he wanted, and Matthew didn't think the man would hesitate to take out any threats standing in his way. At least with the other cops following them he could focus more on Grace while the others watched their surroundings.

"I'm ready," Grace announced.

He groaned when he looked up to see her long legs clad in skintight black capri leggings that stopped just below her knees, and a blue tank top that molded to her prefect breasts and made her eyes shine like sapphires. "How do you manage to look just as sexy in workout clothes as you did in the bikini?"

"It's a gift," she said with a giggle.

Sliding his cell phone into his pocket, Matthew hoped the t-shirt covered the bulge of his weapon. No way was he going anywhere unarmed until they had Emmanuel in custody. He locked up and they walked side by side down the garden path. As soon as they reached the sidewalk Grace gave him a smug smile.

"I might have forgotten to mention I'm a really fast runner. I don't like it but I'm good at it, first one there gets to choose dinner." Grace took off with a burst of speed he hadn't been expecting, leaving him standing there watching her with his mouth hanging open.

The sexy little minx had surprised him again, and he had no doubt that she was going to beat him.

~

9:39 P.M.

Grace yawned. Her eyes were heavy, it was getting harder and harder to keep them open. The nightmares last night had meant she hadn't gotten much sleep, and the weight of trying to figure out what she knew but didn't know she knew was wearing her down. She really had no idea what movie they were watching, but she didn't want it to end because that meant she'd have to go to bed, and she was afraid of more nightmares.

Nightmares sucked, but she had long since accepted they were a part of her life.

Another yawn almost split her face in two and she rubbed at her bleary eyes.

It would be so nice to close them, rest for a while, but she was delaying sleep for as long as humanly possible.

When she yawned for the third time, Matthew picked up the remote and switched the TV off. "Time for bed," he announced.

"We didn't finish the movie," she protested.

"I'll give you twenty dollars right now if you can tell me the name of the movie we're watching. No, better than that, I'll let you pick every dinner for the next week if you can tell me." Matthew made a face like he was making a supreme sacrifice and she laughed.

"Hey, I chose steaks for dinner."

"Yeah, after you made me think you were picking salad."

"I couldn't resist, you looked so disappointed when I bypassed the meat section to go to fresh fruits and vegetables." She had of course beaten him to the supermarket. She might hate running but she was fast, and she knew she'd beaten Matthew for real, although the head start had helped. He'd been right though, she'd needed a physical outlet, and running had done the trick, helping her to feel more settled even if she was still obsessing over her memories.

"You're a sneaky little thing," he teased. His hands circled her ankles and moved her feet from where they were resting on his lap, then he stood and scooped her into his arms.

"I can walk you know, I have legs."

"Long, toned legs to die for, I know, trust me, I've seen them."

And just like that she wasn't so sleepy anymore.

Now she was restless and needy.

But it was too soon.

Wasn't it?

What exactly was it that she was waiting for?

In the few days since she'd met him, they'd bonded, there was no denying it, just like there was no denying that both of them wanted more. Already she felt more of a connection between the two of them than she'd felt with any of her other boyfriends. She couldn't see the future, she didn't even know if she'd be alive let alone whether things worked out between her and Matthew, but did she really want to miss out on the opportunity to have him now?

The future was uncertain at best. Shouldn't she take hold of the here and now?

Time was an arbitrary concept anyway. Some people met, had a whirlwind romance, and were still happily married at the end of their lives. Other people met, dated for years, had a long engagement, and were divorced within a year.

It was time to trust her gut and her gut said Matthew was a man who would always put her first. He made her laugh, spending time with him was easy, they got along, and she really liked him a lot. There was nothing wrong with her doing something about it.

Why was she trying to convince herself of that?

They were two consenting adults. They could have sex if they wanted to.

While she'd been trying to figure things out, Matthew had checked the locks, switched off the lights, and carried her upstairs to her bedroom. He set her on her feet and then touched a tender kiss to her forehead.

"Sweet dreams, sweetheart."

"Matthew, wait." She grabbed his hand when he went to turn, she wasn't ready for him to go yet.

"What do you want, curly?" He kept his hands by his sides, and she could tell he was doing his best to appear as non-threatening as possible. If Matthew was putting the ball in her court, then she was picking up said ball and volleying it.

"I want you." Grace had never been particularly forward when it came to men, but Matthew was different. What she felt for him was different. Somehow those strong feelings made her more confident.

"Are you sure?"

"Would I have said it if I didn't mean it?" Taking Matthew's hand, she led him over to the bed. Slowly she lifted her t-shirt over her head, letting it fall to the floor, then she hooked her fingers into the waistband of her leggings and shimmied them down her legs. She stood before him in nothing but her panties.

Heat practically poured off Matthew, but he still didn't move.

All his honor and self-control made her want to shatter it.

Stepping closer she smiled when she saw Matthew's hungry gaze tracking her every move. This time her hands went to the hem of his t-shirt, and she pushed it up, and he helped pull it over his head.

"Wow," she murmured. He really was cut. His muscles were so sculpted that she couldn't help but run her fingers across each ridge and plane. At her touch, she could see him growing hard, his length standing to attention, and she ran the tip of one finger along it, making Matthew hiss in a breath.

"You keep tempting me like that, sweetheart, and I won't be able to restrain myself," he warned.

"Good. I don't want your restraint right now."

Matthew groaned and wrapped his hands around her hips, and he lifted her, rubbing her center along his length, and ripping a moan from her lips.

"These have got to go," Matthew said as he set her on her feet and slid the panties down her legs. "These legs look even better when you have nothing else on. And these breasts." He palmed them, his fingers kneaded her sensitive flesh, then he swirled the pad of a finger over her nipples, making them pebble. "I can't wait to taste them," he said as he scooped her up and laid her down on the bed. Before touching her, he stood above her, his eyes sweeping over her naked body, spread out before him. Everywhere his gaze touched her body responded until all of her was tingling, heated with a flush that there was only one way to put out.

"Hurry up and touch me," she pleaded because she absolutely wasn't above begging right now. If he didn't touch her soon, she was going to burn from the inside out.

"Oh, I intend to, honey. I'm going to touch every inch of you with my fingers, and then my tongue, and then I'm going to bury myself inside you and you're going to come so hard you're going to think you lost your mind."

"I think I already lost my mind," she murmured.

The smile he gave her was pure sex and her insides clenched in delightful anticipation.

Then his fingers slipped between her legs, and he was right, the ability to think suddenly fled.

All she could do was feel.

Feel the heat building low in her stomach as his thumb slid in slow circles on her needy little bundle of nerves. A finger brushed at her entrance and inched inside her so slowly she thought she was going to die from the desire to feel him inside her body.

Once he had one finger buried deep, he added another, the pressure of his thumb increased, and the heat growing inside her began to burn so brightly she felt like she was smoldering. Then his body moved to stretch out above her, and his lips closed around one of her nipples. The heat of his mouth, the rasp of his teeth, and the swirl of his tongue added to what his very expert hand was doing between her legs lit the match and finally set her alight.

She came long and hard, so hard in fact it felt like flames were shooting through her body like a mess of shooting stars.

Grace was still floating back down to earth when Matthew shed his shorts and settled between her legs.

Like a flip was switched, her hazy afterglow morphed into terror.

"Hold her down. Stop fighting me, Grace. This is happening whether you want it or not, I did my time, now you owe me."

"Grace! Sweetheart, what's wrong? It's okay, honey, it's okay. We won't do anything you don't want to."

She hadn't even realized she was screaming no and fighting him until he hauled her into his lap and began to touch soft kisses to the top of her head.

"Matthew?"

"Right here, honey."

Mortification washed over her.

She'd freaked out, had a flash back, right after he'd given her an earth-shattering orgasm. When he went to initiate sex, her brain must have transported itself back to the night of her rape. How embarrassing. How was she ever going to look Matthew in the eye ever again?

"Stop that," he admonished.

"Stop what?" she asked weakly, feeling spent and shaky.

"Whatever is running through your head and making you look that distraught. It's okay, Grace."

"It's not, I freaked out."

"Which is perfectly fine. Maybe we rushed things a little too much."

"No, I wanted this," she assured him. "So much. I don't know what happened."

"You've been through so much and living with the threat of Emmanuel hanging over your head isn't helping. How about I tuck you in and you get yourself some rest."

Grace grabbed at him. She didn't want to be alone. "Stay, please."

"I don't want to freak you out again."

"You won't. Just stay, please. Hold me, I ... I need you to hold me tonight ... please."

"Oh, honey, you never ever have to ask me to be there for you. I would love to hold you tonight."

Matthew moved them both so they were lying down, him on his back, her on her side, tucked against him, her cheek pillowed on his chest. His arm wrapped around her, holding her snug at his side, and he covered them both with the blankets.

"Night, Matthew," she said, suddenly exhausted.

His lips touched her forehead, hovering there for a moment. "Sweet dreams, sweetheart. I've got you."

Yeah, he did.

He hadn't gotten angry at her for freaking out right in the middle of sex. He hadn't run from the room or looked at her like she was crazy, instead, he'd done the opposite. There had been understanding in his eyes, concern too, but not the patronizing kind. And he was still here, holding her in his arms. He was a good guy, and with him beside her she might actually manage to sleep without the nightmares tonight.

CHAPTER
Eight

July 13th
2:16 A.M.

Something woke him.

It took Matthew a few moments to figure out what it was. It wasn't the beautiful woman snuggled at his side, Grace had been sleeping peacefully ever since he'd tucked her against him, like her brain had been waiting for a safehold so it could let go and finally get the rest it needed. He'd been majorly unprepared for her meltdown right in the middle of making out. She'd had no problem with his fingers between her legs, it wasn't until he went to thrust inside her tight, wet heat that she'd freaked.

It hadn't gone unnoticed that when he touched her as a lover would she'd been fine, but when he'd gone to have sex with her—as someone touching her against her will might—she'd snapped.

Further proof there was something she was still holding back.

If it wasn't Grace who had awakened him then it was something else.

Matthew carefully reached out and grabbed his cell phone from the nightstand. There were no alerts, so he knew the house's security system hadn't been breached. There weren't any calls or texts from the team watching the house either. So what had woken him?

A gentle breeze wafted through the open bedroom window and he knew.

Smell.

Even in sleep his nose had picked up on the smell of smoke and alerted his brain that it needed to do something about it.

"Grace, wake up," he said, giving her a shake as he hurried out of the bed and to the window, confirming his worst fears. The house across the street where the pair of cops watching the house were staying was up in flames.

Neither of them had contacted him, were they already dead?

And why had Emmanuel gone after them instead of going straight for Grace.

Maybe the man was smarter than they'd given him credit for. Yes, he'd obviously managed to track Grace down, but he wasn't so desperate—at least not yet—to go straight for her. Instead, he'd taken out the threat first.

Well, one of the threats because he was still here and if Emmanuel wanted Grace, the man was going to have to get past him first.

"Grace," he called again as he began to get dressed.

She stirred and turned in the direction of his voice. "Matthew?"

"Get up, sweetheart."

"What's going on?" She blinked sleepily at him as she sat up, looking all adorable and sleep rumpled. This wasn't how he'd wanted to start their day. He'd thought he would wake her with a kiss, they'd talk if Grace was up to it, or they'd just enjoy hanging by the pool as they had the last few days.

"I need you to get up and get dressed as quickly as you can, then grab your purse." Suitcases they could come back for later, but he wanted her to have her cell phone on her at all times.

"Why? What's wrong? Is he here?" she asked, fear in her voice now as she scrambled out of the bed and began throwing on clothes.

"Yes, but not in the house, the house where our back up is watching us is on fire."

"On fire?" she squeaked, pausing with one leg in her leggings and one out.

"No doubt a trap," he told her, putting on his shoes. All he could think about was how he had to move her. It was one thing to allow Grace to play bait when they had back up to watch out for them, completely another when it was just him and a man who was an unusual mix of carefully controlled and prepared, and cruelly insane. "We have to get out of here."

"What? No." Grace pulled back when he shoved her shoes and purse at her and began to tug her toward the door. "This is why we're here, to draw him out."

"Right, but now it's just the two of us," he reminded her.

"You can take him."

"While I appreciate the vote of confidence, curly, I can't risk your life like that. Emmanuel has a plan, he's not just going to come blindly in here. The fire was a trap, it separates us, evens the odds in his favor. I'd bet anything he has a plan for how to get me out of the way."

Grace paled. "You think he'll kill you?"

"Not if I have anything to say about it. But he's playing this smart which means we have to as well."

"So, we're running?" Grace balanced on one foot and slipped on one of her shoes, and then did the other one.

"We're strategically retreating and regrouping, then we'll take another go at this. I promise you, we aren't giving up."

Hand in hand they made their way downstairs. Matthew had his gun in his free hand, and his cell phone was in his pocket, there were still no alerts telling him that Emmanuel had gotten inside the house.

Still, he couldn't help but feel on edge.

Something felt wrong.

Matthew opened the garage door, ushered Grace into the passenger seat then hurried into the driver's seat. They had to get out of here. Whatever Emmanuel was planning, he couldn't allow it to work. Playing games, using Grace as bait was one thing. But this had quickly gotten out of hand, and he wouldn't risk her life. Once he got her someplace safe, they'd call in back up and then move somewhere else. It would mean starting over, waiting for Emmanuel to find them again, but this time they'd be more prepared.

"Stop," Grace ordered as he pulled out of the driveway.

"What?"

"We can't leave them."

"Leave who?"

"The cops. They're trapped in there, otherwise they'd have come to help us. We can't leave them." Her blue eyes pleaded with him.

"Fire department will be here soon."

"What if it's not soon enough? Please, Matthew, I can't let anyone else die because of me. I can't. Please."

Her pain was like a physical thing, filling the car's interior. How could he say no to her? "You drive out of here then. I don't want you getting hurt. For all we know this was his plan. Set the fire, wait for me to go to help, leaving you alone and vulnerable. I won't let him get you, Grace, not for anything. So, you drive to the gas station around the corner. Go inside and wait for me, call 911, and explain what's going on."

"Thank you." She leaned across the center console to kiss him, and he curled his hands into her hair and held her there, deepening the kiss. "Be safe," she said when he released her.

"You too."

Even though it felt wrong, he got out of the car and watched as Grace climbed over the console and into the driver's seat. It wasn't until she had driven off down the street and he was certain no one had driven off after her, that he turned and hurried toward the house.

The fire was raging, but it was burning slowly, it didn't look like an accelerant had been used. Chances were, Emmanuel hadn't come with the plan of setting a fire. He'd obviously tracked Grace here, then watched for a while, noticed that the house opposite the safehouse had cops in it and decided to get them out of the way. If he hadn't planned on starting a fire, what did he use to set it?

Was Emmanuel a smoker?

No, Grace would have mentioned that.

One of the cops providing back up was a smoker though, chain smoked a dozen packs a day. Had Emmanuel used Officer Lennon's lighter?

Scanning the garden, he noticed a lump near the hedges, so he headed in that direction. As he neared it, he saw it was the two officers, both were unconscious, blood on their heads, but when he checked their pulses both were strong. From the looks of things, Emmanuel must have lured one of the cops out, then knocked him unconscious, then waited for the partner or roused him on the radio, and taken him out too.

They'd made a dangerous mistake, underestimated their opponent, and it very nearly could have ended in disaster.

People were spilling out of houses, and he moved so he could keep watch over the two injured cops while he waited for fire trucks and ambulances to arrive. He sent a text to Heidi, and one to Grace's brother Elijah, letting them know what was going on. They were going to need to regroup, come up with a better plan. He still believed that using Grace as bait was the fastest way to end this, but if she wound up getting hurt he was never going to forgive himself.

Grace had wriggled right through the impenetrable defenses he'd thought he had around his heart with her haunted but determined baby blues, and her stubborn resolve to rebuild her life. Her strength was beautiful, inspiring, and humbling, and he knew he could easily be persuaded to spend the rest of his life worshipping her beautiful body and soul. But to do that he had to keep her alive.

Something he was starting to think wasn't going to be all that easy to do.

~

2:33 A.M.

It made her feel like a coward to run.

The only reason Grace had left was because she recognized that without any training, she was more a liability than she was a help.

Still, it sucked.

Her fingers drummed on the steering wheel as she stopped at a red light. Being still made her anxious. She'd spent years stuck in that house, nowhere to go, nothing to do, and no way to fight back against the man who controlled her every move. Now she was filled with a need to be doing something.

Problem was there was nothing for her to do.

Nothing but run and hide.

The light turned green, and her hands tightened around the wheel, wishing it was Emmanuel's throat instead. How many times had she wished she could kill him? The thought had been a near daily companion, but the metal cuff around her ankle, attached to a chain that kept her tethered to the floor limited her options. Emmanuel never allowed the key that would free her to be within her reach, it was his safety backup plan. Killing him meant ending her own life, only it would be a horrible, slow death. Her only option would have been to cut off her own foot, and while she absolutely would have done it—she would have done anything to get free—he never gave her anything sharp enough to do it.

She'd been trapped.

Helpless.

But she wasn't anymore, and she never would be again.

The gas station appeared up ahead, and Grace scanned the quiet street behind her. There was no one there, at least no one that she could see. Every few seconds she scanned her surroundings, sure that she would see Emmanuel coming for her, but so far she hadn't. It could be because he was still back at the house, or he was following her but in a way she hadn't anticipated.

She wished Matthew was here. Was he okay?

If he got hurt, or worse killed because of her it was going to snap the thin string of control she was using to keep her emotions in check.

The string was wobbling, slipping, getting dangerously close to coming undone. Last night had given her a little taste of what would happen if she ever let the string fall completely. It was one of the reasons she had so readily agreed to play bait. Each thing she did that helped her take a step forward—getting a job, going back to school, getting her own place, and definitely helping put her abductor behind bars—was like tying another knot in that string. The more knots the less the chances the string could unravel.

With a sigh, Grace pulled into the gas station, parking her car as close to the store as she could so her car was bathed in light. Maybe her life would never be normal, never be what it could have been if Emmanuel had never kidnapped her, but it didn't mean her life couldn't still be happy. Matthew made her happy, she hoped he wasn't going to leave once this was over and she was safe.

She was pretty sure her heart couldn't cope with that.

Turning the engine off she glanced around. There hadn't been another car pull in after her, and if Emmanuel was following her on a bike or something then she would have noticed it. Matthew had told her to go inside and call 911, but when she went to open the door she saw shadows moving in the far corner of the gas station.

Emmanuel?

Grace slipped her phone out of her purse and was dialing 911 when she saw someone walking toward her. Unbuckling her seatbelt, she scrunched down in her seat. Maybe if she hid then whoever it was wouldn't realize she was there.

No doubt she was being paranoid, there was no way to know that the person had anything to do with her. In fact, it was unlikely they had anything to do with her.

Yet she could hear footsteps.

She slipped down onto the floor. This couldn't be happening again. No way would she survive again in Emmanuel's house.

Shadows moved above her.

A figure appeared in the passenger window.

Someone was opening the door.

Why was this happening to her again?

Fear threatened to paralyze her, but then a heavy dose of anger hit.

How dare Emmanuel think of her as just a toy in his game. She wasn't a toy, she was a person with her own thoughts and emotions, her own wants and needs, and she'd been victimized enough. She wanted her chance with Matthew, surely she deserved it after everything she had been through.

As the passenger door opened, Grace threw open the driver's door and scrambled out. There was no way she was going down without a fight.

Grace took off at a run toward the street. If it was Emmanuel—and she couldn't think of anyone else who would be trying to get into Matthew's car—then he would expect her to run toward the store not away from it. But if she got to the street then she could hide in a front yard, call the cops, and then text Matthew and let him know where she was.

It sounded so easy, but as she took off running, she heard footsteps behind her.

No.

She couldn't go back.

A hand closed around her shoulder, and she flung out a fist as she was spun around.

"Whoa, Gracie, easy, sweetie. It's only me."

"Elijah," she said on a shudder. "Don't do that to me." She swung a fist at his shoulder and threw her entire bodyweight into it.

Her brother grunted as her fist connected. "Ow, Gracie."

"You deserved it," she muttered. "You scared me almost to death. I thought you were Emmanuel. Why didn't you say anything?"

"I thought you were inside."

"Then why were you at the car?"

"I was going to check it for trackers, see if Emmanuel had planted one on there at some point."

"You could have called out when you chased me." She huffed, but even though he'd about given her a heart attack she was glad to see him. "How did you know I was here?"

"Matthew texted. Ali and I came right over," Elijah explained.

"Elijah, she's not inside," Ali called out as she came rushing out of the store.

"It's, okay, I got her, she was hiding in the car," Elijah assured his wife.

"Gracie, you okay?" Ali pulled her in for a hug.

She held on a little tighter than she probably should have given that she was trying really hard to be independent and not fall into the helpless baby sister role that she knew her brothers would be all too happy with. Grace knew they wanted to see her grow strong again, but she also knew they needed to try to make up for what they thought of as their failures in finding her. They would have to try to figure out a middle ground, something that allowed all of them to get what they needed. But for now, what she needed was the safety of her family's presence.

"I'm okay," she assured her sister-in-law. "What about Matthew and the cops at the house? The fire? Do you know if they're all okay?"

"I haven't heard yet," Elijah replied. "Come on, let's get you into our car, we'll drive to the station, keep you there until we figure out what to do next."

What they were going to do next was find another safehouse, leak its location again, and then wait for Emmanuel to come back. There was no way she was giving up. Only this time they would have to make sure they had enough cops watching to make sure Emmanuel couldn't play more games.

She was so sick of his games.

Before she could say that her phone rang, and she quickly pulled it from her purse, worried it was bad news. Matthew's name was on the screen and her hand was shaking as she accepted the call. "Matthew?"

"Hey, honey, I called as soon as I could. Are you okay?"

"Are *you* okay?"

"Fire is out. The other cops weren't in the house. The fire department is here, and cops. I'm going to come to you as soon as I can."

Grace wanted to beg him to come quickly, but she couldn't allow herself to rely on him too much. She liked him, hoped they had a future, but she had learned that when it came down to it, the only person you could ever truly rely upon was yourself. That was why she had to get strong, why she had to learn how to defend herself, why she had to survive. Still ...

"Be safe, Matthew, Emmanuel could still be around, I don't want him to hurt you."

"He won't hurt me, Grace."

Of course he couldn't know that.

"I'll be careful, I promise," Matthew said. "Now promise me the same."

She gave a small smile even though he couldn't see her. "I promise. And, Matthew?"

"Yeah, curly?"

"Hurry."

"Sweetheart, trust me, I'm hurrying."

As she ended the call, Grace couldn't help but wonder if maybe it wasn't a weakness to need someone if they needed you just as badly.

~

5:50 A.M.

He opened his arms and Grace didn't hesitate to walk into them.

The second he had her wrapped in an embrace, Matthew finally felt himself settle.

Grace was safe, alive, uninjured, and yet he couldn't help but feel like Emmanuel had taken another piece of her soul with his latest stunt. When everyone else left the new safehouse they needed to talk. She was holding back, and while she was entitled to keep anything not pertaining to finding Emmanuel to herself if she chose, whatever she was keeping to herself was hurting her. The nightmares and her breakdown when they'd been in bed were proof of that.

Earning her trust was important to him, and he wanted her to know that there wasn't anything she couldn't tell him.

"You're okay," Grace murmured, voice muffled as her face pressed against his chest. "I was scared."

"I wouldn't have let him hurt you," he promised, tightening his hold on her.

She lifted her head and looked up at him. "Scared for *you*."

Such simple words and yet they latched on to a place deep inside of him. It had been a long time since anyone had cared that deeply about him. Perhaps even the first time. Grace had given him a gift he had no intention of squandering.

Brushing his fingertips across her pale cheeks, he leaned down and touched his forehead to hers. "I won't let anything happen to me either," he promised. Not a vow he made lightly. He had a feeling losing him would hurt Grace as badly as losing her would hurt him. They'd both been through enough. It was time for people to stop messing with their happiness and let them finally find peace.

"So, this is the new safehouse, huh?" Grace asked as she stepped out of his embrace but didn't move away from his side.

"And this time we have a whole lot more people watching over you," Elijah informed her.

The Bennetts had gone all out calling in favors from family and friends. Elijah and his partner would be watching the house, Alayna and her partner, Allina and Jonathon. Jonathon's brother-in-law Nick and his partner, Jonathon's sister-in-law Naomi and her husband Sam, who were both highly trained bodyguards, and Rylla and her husband Nate, who worked with Sam and Naomi at their private security firm. That made twelve people in addition to the cops assigned to watch the place.

No one was getting in here.

No one.

Emmanuel was going to realize that when he made another play to get to Grace.

"Doesn't mean Emmanuel won't get me," Grace said softly. Almost acceptingly, and that made him angrier than if she'd said it with anger directed at them for almost failing her this morning.

"He can't have you, Grace," he said firmly, infusing every bit of confidence he felt of the team's ability to protect her into his tone so she would believe it.

The smile she gave him wasn't quite patronizing, but it was a little indulgent as though she thought his effort was sweet but didn't necessarily agree. "Well at least we've done everything we can do."

"If you want to go to a real safehouse, Gracie, we'll make it happen," Ali said.

"No. I want this to end. I can't rebuild my life until I know Emmanuel is no longer a threat, and I want my life back. Emmanuel has taken enough from me. He's not going to take my future too." Grace's voice was firm, steady, no trace of the fear he knew she was feeling.

"Grace needs some rest," he said, wanting to get her alone.

"We're all right outside, you're safe, protected, not alone this time," Jeremiah reminded her.

After hugging and reassuring her several times over, her family finally left and then it was just the two of them. Unsure how to ask her to open up to him, trust him, let him in so he knew how best to support her, instead he locked up, set the alarm, and then took her hand. "You want something to eat, or do you want to go back to bed, try to get some sleep?"

Grace shrugged, and he sensed her restlessness. If he had to guess, Matthew thought she wanted to spill all to him, but wasn't sure how to go about it. Whatever she was keeping back was something big, and he was sure that Emmanuel had in fact molested her despite her repeated denials.

"How about we just sit, watch a movie, relax?" he suggested, guiding her into the living room where a large screen TV took up most of one wall.

No sooner had he sat them both down on the couch and switched on the TV, browsing through Netflix to find something to watch, than Grace blurted out, "I was raped."

He stilled. Felt fury rush through him. Did his best to remain calm because the last thing Grace needed was to think the rage inside him was in any way directed at her. "I'm going to kill Emmanuel when we finally catch him."

"Matthew, it wasn't him. I told you he didn't touch me like that. I think in his delusional mind he truly believed he was helping me by teaching me his lessons."

She'd been in the hospital, her family surrounding her around the clock, then at her brother's house, again never left alone, and then with him at the safehouse, so he knew that it hadn't happened to her since she'd been rescued. "Before?"

"Yes, about two months before Emmanuel abducted me."

She was sitting stiffly, almost like she was braced for an attack of some sort. If she expected him to be angry with her that she had been assaulted, then he was offended. He would never blame a victim for something outside of their control. Curling an arm around her shoulders, he eased her sideways so she was curled up against him. She came reluctantly at first, but then the tension seemed to drain out of her, and she sagged against him.

Keeping his voice calm, he began to stroke his fingers through her curls. "Tell me what happened, sweetheart."

Like she'd been desperate to unload this burden but had been holding back, words began to pour out of her. "There was this guy who was in my classes, we were study partners. He'd asked me out earlier in the semester and I said no because I'd just broken up with my boyfriend who had cheated on me, and while I was over him, I wasn't ready for a relationship. He seemed cool with it, and we were friends. At least I thought we were. One night he invited me to a party. I didn't want to go because he would be the only one there that I knew, but we'd just handed in a major assignment and I needed to blow off a little steam, so I went. It was okay at first, but then I started feeling weird, he must have slipped something in my drink. I knew something was wrong, I should have called one of my brothers, or Ali or Laynie, but I didn't. I should have called a cab or something, but I didn't do that either. My memories are a little hazy after that, but I remember being taken upstairs. I remember three men, two of them held me down while the one I thought was my friend raped me. I must have passed out at some point because the next thing I remember is waking up at home in my bed."

It took substantial effort to not hit something.

The only reason he held back was because he was sure Grace would interpret his anger as being directed at her, he could hear the recrimination in her voice.

"Did you report it?" he asked.

Grace shuddered against him. "No. I had no proof. I knew he'd drugged me, it would all be he said, she said, and everyone on campus knew that we were friends. I didn't think anyone would believe me."

There was shame in her voice now, and that about snapped his control. How many times had he heard victims of sexual assault say those exact same things? They didn't report it because they didn't think they would be believed. He wished with everything he was that they lived in a world where victims were always given the benefit of the doubt without that privilege being handed to their assailants.

"I hate that happened to you, Grace, and that you felt like you wouldn't be believed. I believe you."

Another shudder rippled through her. "Thank you."

"Don't thank me for that, baby. Of course I believe you. I will always believe you and I will always be on your side."

She touched a kiss to his jaw, and he could feel the wetness of her tears. His sweet Grace was finally allowing herself to cry for everything she had been through. "I tried to pretend it never happened, but I wasn't sleeping, was barely eating, and couldn't concentrate on anything. I was withdrawing from my friends, constantly felt like I was in danger, and lived in constant fear of seeing him again. I knew I couldn't go on like that. I called Jem, I thought since he was a psychiatrist, he was the best person to tell, but he was away working a case, and even though I left a message he never called me back. So, I reached out to one of those sexual assault helplines, spoke to someone there. It helped, a lot, and I knew I needed to tell my family and report it, even if he was never prosecuted, I needed to do it for me. Before I could, Emmanuel broke into my house and abducted me."

Once again, Matthew found himself in awe of her strength and bravery. She was the very definition of a survivor, whatever was thrown at her, however bad it got, no matter what she had to do, she fought to survive. "I'm so proud of you, baby."

Her tears were coming faster now, harder, and she shook her head vehemently. "At first, when I woke up in Emmanuel's house of horrors, I wondered if it was a punishment. What if Dave raped someone else because I didn't turn him in? It would be my fault. I should have done the right thing, gone straight to the cops, reported what happened. If I could go back and do it over then I would. I swear I would. I don't want to be punished anymore for keeping quiet. I just want it to be over, Matthew. I want it to be finished, whatever finished looks like."

She broke down then, her tears became a flood, and he felt his heart breaking right along with hers. Scooping her up, he pulled her onto his lap, and folded his body around her as though he could protect her from the pain. He rocked her, stroked her back, held her, murmured a string of nonsense consolations in her ear, and felt more helpless than he ever had before in his life.

He wanted to do what nobody had ever done for him, he wanted to take away her bad memories, protect her, keep her safe, and save her. He wanted to be her soft place to fall. One thing he knew with absolute certainty, this woman owned him, body, heart, and soul. Forever.

~

6:19 A.M.

The sobs emanated from a place deep inside her. A place that had been shredded when Dave had raped her, those pieces chopped up further when Emmanuel had kidnapped her and used her to play out his own sick fantasies.

Ever since Matthew had walked into that house of horrors and rescued her, she had been fighting her feelings. Refusing to cry because she thought it would weaken her determination not to let Emmanuel take anything else from her.

She'd been wrong.

So very wrong.

The tears that flowed from her eyes now felt freeing.

They washed away the worst of the pain. They couldn't take it all of course, but they took enough of it that she felt like she could breathe again.

Matthew didn't blame her for being stupid the night she'd been raped, and he hadn't reprimanded her for not running straight to the cops to report it. He hadn't even told her she was stupid for thinking that Emmanuel's fable games were her punishment for not doing what she had to to make sure Dave couldn't hurt another woman.

No, he did none of that. He just held her tight, cocooning her in a little bundle of warmth and safety, a security that had been lacking from her world for far too long. Her tears didn't scare him, in fact, he seemed to be trying to absorb them if the protective way he was curled around her was any indication.

It was in this moment that Grace knew for certain.

She was falling in love with Detective Matthew Greer.

It was the last thing she had expected to happen when she woke up in a hospital bed and realized her ordeal was over, but it was exactly what had happened.

Somehow, he'd managed to make her feel safe, make her feel understood, and made her feel special, all without seemingly putting any effort into it.

Her parents had shared the kind of love that fairytales, and songs, and romance books were about. They had clicked from the moment they met, nurtured that love over a lifetime, and even if her mom hadn't had a stroke, Grace knew she would never have moved on from dad. The connection they shared was too strong, it was eternal, unbreakable, and strong enough to survive anything.

Was that the kind of love that she and Matthew could share if they nurtured it, tended to it, and helped it to grow?

All of a sudden, she was filled with a burning need to be possessed by the man holding her with such tenderness and care. She wanted all of him, wanted to give him all of herself. While she trusted Matthew, her family, and the cops to do everything they could to protect her from Emmanuel, she was also realistic enough to know it might not be enough. He might get his hands on her, might kill her, or keep her locked up for the rest of her life, but there was one thing he couldn't take from her.

Matthew.

Placing her hands on his shoulders, she moved so she was straddling him, and crushed her mouth to his.

He kissed her back for a moment, then pulled back, surprised. "Grace?"

"I want you, now, please." There was a desperation she hadn't felt before in her life, it wasn't just a want for him, it was an all-encompassing need. A need she still didn't quite understand.

"Grace ..." There was a hesitation there, and she got it. Last time they'd made out she'd ruined it by freaking out right in the middle of things. No doubt he was worried about a repeat, but for the first time in almost six years she finally felt free of what Dave had done to her.

"It's okay," she assured him, twirling her fingers through his hair, "I want this, I'm ready for it. I wasn't last time because I hadn't been honest with you. It's been a really long time since it happened, almost six years, I know most of that time I was being kept prisoner, but I'm ready for this. I need it. I need you. Please."

The whispered plea was obviously the straw that broke the camel's back because Matthew pulled her closer, and when his lips met hers again the kiss was possessive. She liked the idea of that, belonging to Matthew, but only because unlike with Emmanuel she knew that Matthew would belong to her too. This wasn't one sided, this time the balance of power was even, they would be partners in this relationship.

When her hands went to unbuckle the jeans he had changed into somewhere between them fleeing the bedroom and arriving at the safe-house, his hands caught hers, stilling them. "No."

"But I thought ..."

He cut her off with another possessive kiss. "Not here, not like this. I want our first time to be special, and for that we need a bed."

Since she couldn't argue with that, she allowed him to gather her up, and carry her up the stairs. As he did, she touched soft kisses to his neck, his chiseled jawline, his face, and finally as they entered the bedroom, his lips.

Matthew set her on her feet, and both of them made quick work of stripping out of their clothes, and then he was standing before her, his hands and his gaze roving her body, leaving trails of the sweetest fire everywhere they went.

"You're so beautiful," he whispered.

"I have scars," she reminded him, suddenly self-conscious of them.

"The story of your survival," he said the leaned down to kiss one on her shoulder. "I want to touch every one of them, replace their pain with pleasure."

He did just that, kneeling before her and working his way down her front touching his lips to each of the scars on her chest, her stomach, her arms, and then the ones of her breasts, finishing off with the lightest of kisses to her pebbled nipples.

"Turn around," he ordered, his voice husky with a sexiness that had her growing wet between the legs.

As though sensing her growing need as he turned her and began to kiss the scars on her back, including the still healing wounds from

Emmanuel's last punishment, he circled one arm in front of her and let his fingers get busy between her legs. By the time he had soothed some of the mental anguish that the wounds that caused the scars had brought her with his kisses, her legs were quivering, pleasure shimmering just out of reach.

"I want to taste you, Grace, may I?" he asked as he stood, his mouth millimeters from her ear.

She shivered at the heat that curled around her skin, somehow finding its way inside her, and fanning the flames of her growing pleasure. "I've never done that before."

"If you don't like it, I'll stop, I promise, but I've been dying to taste you since I saw you in that bikini."

His hand resting low of her stomach he guided her to the bed, turned her around, and laid her on her back so she was lying with her knees hanging over the side of the mattress. His dark head went between her spread legs as he knelt before her, and she almost unraveled just from the heat of his breath against her most intimate area.

That first sweep of his tongue had her gasping, her hips rising of their own accord.

"You like that, huh?" he asked with a wickedly sexy smirk that did weird things to her insides.

"Yes," she whispered.

"Watch me, Grace. Watch and see how much I love tasting you."

Like her eyes were glued to his, she watched in fascinated wonder as his tongue swept along her center before his lips surrounded her pulsing little bundle of nerves and suckled on it. His hands curled under her bottom, lifting her slightly and then his tongue was stabbing at her center, then lapping at her before circling her hard little bud.

It didn't take long before the world began to shimmer in a mass of colors that looked brighter than she'd ever seen, and then she was screaming his name as those colors exploded in a fiery display of ecstasy that fired through her, leaving no part of her untouched.

She was still riding that high as he moved her so she was laid out on the bed, her head on the pillows, and settled between her legs. "Are you sure, Grace?" he asked as he slid on a condom.

"Yes, I'm sure."

Grace cried out as he speared into her in one thrust, stretching her, filling her. There was a moment of pain as her body acclimatized to the feel of his huge length, but it quickly faded, replaced by a pleasure she couldn't even put into words.

"You okay?" he asked, unmoving.

"I'm perfect," she said, reaching for his hands and linking their fingers together.

Their mouths joined, tongues clashing as Grace met Matthew thrust for thrust. Pleasure built anew, growing until it was almost painful, almost unbearable before shattering her into a million pieces when the wall broke and it crashed over her like a tidal wave.

She knew Matthew reached his own peak because his whole body shuddered as his thrusts increased, spurring on her pleasure until she was almost dizzy with it.

Finally, that pleasure began to fade, and Matthew opened his eyes, meeting hers and holding her gaze captive. "My sweet, beautiful, strong survivor," he whispered, and she felt the love in his voice even if he didn't say the word.

"Yours," she agreed.

"Mine," he echoed. "Always mine."

In belonging to a man she cared so much for, who she was already falling in love with, Grace found a safety and a peace she had longed for for so many years. "Mine," she whispered, wrapping her arms around him and drawing him close. He was hers and she wasn't ever letting go.

CHAPTER
Nine

July 14th
4:07 A.M.

This morning he knew exactly what had woken him, and he didn't like it.

Matthew shifted to reach for the cell phone on the nightstand. Unlike yesterday morning when the smell of smoke had come wafting through the open window, taunting him that something might not be right, this morning's wakeup call was like a siren.

"Matt?" Grace asked sleepily as the shrill beep of his phone woke her too.

As he picked up his phone his worst fears were confirmed.

Emmanuel was back.

Only once again he wasn't playing things as they had suspected. Not knowing anything about the man other than what Grace had told them put them at a massive disadvantage. For all they knew Emmanuel was a cop, or in the military, or had some other sort of training. Something that continued to give him the edge while the rest of them played catch up.

"Matt, you're scaring me." Grace had sat up, bringing the sheet with her, holding it clutched around her breasts, and again he wished that this morning he could have woken her up properly. But there would be no making love, no teasing each other over breakfast, no lazy afternoon by the pool.

"Get dressed, sweetheart."

"Again?" Her blue eyes were wide with fear, but she didn't hesitate to do as he'd ordered.

They both got out of bed, threw on the clothes they had discarded last night when he'd carried her upstairs and made sweet love to her before they'd gone to sleep wrapped in each other's arms. It had been the perfect end to perhaps the most perfect day of his life, but then again, he thought that about every day he spent with Grace. Somehow, it just kept getting better and better. After napping, they'd spent the day hanging out inside. Although this safehouse also had a pool, Matthew hadn't wanted her in any danger, so they'd hung out indoors, playing boardgames, watching movies, and talking. For a while they'd both been able to pretend they weren't sitting ducks waiting for danger to come knocking on the door.

But reality was back, and it sucked.

Once they were dressed, he grabbed Grace's purse and once again, just as he had yesterday morning, he thrust it into her arms.

"What's going on? What's he doing this time?" she demanded as he hustled her down the stairs. There was an edge of panic to her voice. This time it wasn't nameless cops out there watching their backs, this time for Grace it was her family, the people she loved the most in the world.

"He's shooting up the street," he told her.

She froze. "I don't hear any gunfire."

"Sniper," he replied, knowing she would know what that meant. She was from a cop family, she would know exactly the danger a sniper presented.

"Is anyone hit?"

"No one's dead," he replied. That was all he was willing to tell her at the moment, but it wasn't much less than what he knew. All the text alert had told him was that a sniper was hitting the street and that there were injuries but no casualties.

At least not yet.

"But at least one person has been hit."

Damn. She was so much more perceptive than he gave her credit for, and he already thought everything about her was pretty amazing.

Hardening his gaze, he resisted the urge to drag her into his arms and reassure her that Emmanuel still wasn't getting to her. That he would stand between her and danger as many times as it took to ensure her safety. "We need to go, Grace. Now."

Although he could tell she wanted to argue, press for details, she didn't. Instead, she allowed him to hurry her the rest of the way down the stairs. Obviously, the plan to have Grace play bait wasn't going to work. Emmanuel wasn't going to do anything unless he was sure he was going to get what he wanted.

What he wanted was Grace, but Emmanuel was going to have to accept that Matthew wanted her more.

"This isn't going to work, is it?" Grace asked in a whisper as they carefully crossed the living room heading for the door to the garage. "It doesn't matter how many people are watching me, waiting to catch him, he's going to hurt or kill whoever stands between us. Matthew, I can't let him hurt you."

"He won't," he vowed, praying like hell he could keep that promise.

"He might."

"He won't."

"He. Might," she said, pulling her arm free from his as he opened the car door and tried to push her into the passenger seat. "I won't let that happen."

The stubborn glint in her eyes almost made him smile. She was adorable when she thought she could protect him. Since he knew showing his amusement that the tiny little thing thought she could stop him from protecting her with his life if it came down to it would only antagonize her, instead he dropped a quick kiss to her lips.

"Get into the car, Grace."

She huffed but did as he asked. "Are we running?" she asked as he climbed into the driver's seat.

"Straight to the precinct."

"We're not going to try playing bait again, are we?" There was resignation in her tone, but she didn't complain or rail at him because things hadn't worked out the way they had all assumed.

"No, honey, we're not. It's too risky. Emmanuel is unpredictable and seems to have more skills than we've given him credit for."

"I'm going to be put in a real safehouse, aren't I?" Again, there was resignation and a tinge of pain in her voice, but she uttered no complaints and didn't scream or throw a tantrum.

"Yes."

"It's exchanging one prison for another."

"At least you'll be alive," he reminded her as he reached over and covered one of her hands which was resting on her thigh.

"At least I'll be alive," she agreed, and turned her hand over so she could lace her fingers with his.

As much as he knew that she would suffer being forced into hiding for real—where there would be no lazing by the pool or runs to the supermarket for dinner—it was really the only option they had left. Emmanuel wasn't going away until he got what he wanted, and there was no way Matthew was letting him get Grace.

Sending a text to let the others know to lay down cover fire, he put the garage door up and threw the car into reverse. Zooming out of the garage and onto the street, he quickly took off up the road while the cops protecting them did the best they could to lay down some cover fire so he could get away.

Of course, laying down covering fire for a sniper, in the middle of suburbia was easier said than done. Matthew had no idea where the sniper was beyond the direction the bullets had been coming from, but there was a large apartment complex just a few blocks over from the safehouse, so he had to presume that Emmanuel had set himself up there.

If that was where Emmanuel was holed up, then as soon as they managed to get out of his range they'd be safe. He'd get Grace to the precinct, she'd remain there until they had a real safehouse secured, then she'd be moved there. There was a chance he wouldn't be allowed to go with her, possibly that none of her family would either which meant to all intents and purposes, she would be right back in the same situation he had rescued her from a week ago.

At least this time she wouldn't be forced to participate in games where you played to the death. Matthew was consoling himself with that fact when the sound of breaking glass surprised him.

A split-second later, pain pierced his chest.

Grace screamed.

The car veered as he lost control of it.

His brain seemed unwilling to provide him with a reason as to why the world was suddenly going black around the edges.

They slammed into something.

More pain.

"Matt?"

Hands touched him.

Sweet, gentle hands.

Grace's hands.

"Matthew, you're going to be okay, I won't let you die," Grace's voice, filled with pain, heavy with tears, insisted and her face moved into his line of sight. She was pressing something against his chest, he could tell only because of the searing pain.

His body was going numb.

His brain threatening to check out.

"Run," he ordered.

"What?"

"Run."

"You're so weak, I can't hear you. Hold on." She moved so her ear was right above his lips. "What did you say?"

"Run."

"I'm not leaving you. You were shot, I have to keep pressure on your wound."

Matthew shook his head.

Didn't she know he would gladly give his life for hers?

All that mattered was that Emmanuel not get his hands on her again.

"He'll be coming. You he wants. Run. Call the others."

"Matthew."

There was so much emotion in that one word, even as the world continued to fade around him he heard it, felt it.

"Grace, run."

Her lips briefly touched his. "I love you, Matthew."

Then she was gone.

He tried to lift his hand, put pressure on his wound, but he was too weak. As the blackness closed in around him, he realized Grace's words would likely be the last he ever heard. As deaths went a declaration of love from the woman he was falling in love with wasn't a bad way to go.

"Love you too," he murmured to the empty car before the blackness dragged him under.

~

4:18 A.M.

Removing her hands from the bleeding wound on Matthew's chest was the hardest thing Grace had ever had to do in her life.

Tears streamed down her face as she stumbled from the car, her knees so weak they would barely support her. Grace just managed not to land hard on her backside and staggered across the road to the sidewalk.

Call for help.

If someone didn't get to Matthew soon, he was going to die.

There was no way she could allow herself to believe that he was already dead.

Her hands shook as she found her cell phone in her purse and pulled it out. She had a pounding headache from the crash, and she was achy and sore all over, no doubt she would have a myriad of bruises come sunrise. Somehow, she managed not to drop the phone onto the concrete and pulled up the first name in the contacts.

"Gracie?" Elijah's anxious voice answered in less than one ring.

The tears came faster at the sound of her brother's voice. Why couldn't this just be over? Why couldn't Emmanuel let her go? Why couldn't they find him and arrest him so he could never hurt her, the people she cared about, or anyone else ever again?

"Gracie, what's wrong?"

"M-Matthew," she managed to get out through her tears.

"What happened to Matthew, sweetie?"

She tried to tell him but all she could think about was the blood.

So much blood.

Matthew was dying, she was sure of it, and it was all her fault. Another death she would have to carry on her conscience. How many other people had been hurt back at the safehouse? Matthew said no one was dead—or at least they hadn't been when she and Matthew had left —but people had been hurt, she knew that. All those people had spouses, children, parents, siblings, friends, they had people who loved them and cared about them and yet they hadn't hesitated to risk their lives to help her.

Now Matthew might die because of that, and so might some of the others.

She was going to be sick.

Dropping to her knees, Grace vomited onto the sidewalk, her stomach cramping painfully as it expelled what little food she'd managed to get down yesterday.

"Gracie, sweetie, tell me what's wrong. Take a deep breath okay, calm yourself down, tell me where you are so I can come and get you." Elijah's calm voice coming through the phone she still clutched tightly in one hand managed to help her get herself somewhat under control.

"He was shot," she choked out. "We crashed the car. He's bleeding a lot, but he told me to run."

"He did the right thing, Gracie, you're the one Emmanuel wants. It's probably safer for Matthew for you not to be near him right now. If Emmanuel checks out the car and you're there he might kill him out of spite."

She hadn't thought of that, and it did go a small way toward easing her guilt for leaving. "You'll send an ambulance to him, right?"

"Of course, sweetie," Elijah soothed. "Do you know where you are?"

"Just a few streets over from the safehouse, not more than five minutes away."

"All right, we're on our way now. I want you to find a place to ..."

His voice faded away as Grace lowered the phone from her ear and looked about. While she couldn't see anything or anyone there had been a change in the atmosphere she couldn't explain. Her gut probably telling her that something wasn't right.

Emmanuel must be coming.

If he'd tracked them through his scope from the safehouse to where he'd shot Matthew, then he knew where they were.

He was coming for her.

Elijah was still talking but she blocked him out as she got up and moved slowly further into the darkness away from the streetlights. The house she'd stopped in front of had several large bushes in its front yard and she crawled toward one of them. All she had to do was stay hidden long enough for Elijah and the others to come for her. It shouldn't take more than about ten minutes, and then help would be here for Matthew, and they'd all go somewhere safe and come up with a different plan to find Emmanuel.

"Gracie! What's going on?"

Realizing she'd been ignoring Elijah's pleas for her to answer him she lifted the phone to her ear again. "I think he's coming," she whispered, her voice a mere hint of a sound. She didn't want to do anything to endanger Matthew more than he already was.

"Okay, sweetie, just hide, and hold on, we're coming."

She could see a shadowy figure dressed all in black walking down the street. The person looked out of place with their black jeans, hoodie, gloves, and baseball cap pulled low to cover his face, the night was hot, the clothing was totally inappropriate. It had to be Emmanuel.

It wasn't until the shadowy black figure moved closer that she saw he wasn't alone.

He had a hand wrapped around the arm of a woman who was gagged, blindfolded, and had her arms pulled and bound behind her.

Grace recognized the woman, it was the one from the house, the last one who had been brought there before Matthew and Rylla had rescued them. The woman hadn't had to play any games yet, so she didn't know just how truly evil Emmanuel was, but it looked like she was about to find out.

"I know you're nearby, Grace," Emmanuel called out, stopping just a few yards away from where she was hiding.

She curled in on herself, trying to make herself as small a target as possible, and held her breath, praying he didn't really know she was close by.

"Come on, Grace, we don't have time for this. Either you come out now or I start shooting Barbara Lack."

All she had to do was stay hidden for a couple more minutes and then her brothers and the others would be here. That was it, surely, he wouldn't shoot the woman in the next few minutes.

"I'm losing patience, Grace. You've only been out of our home for a few days and yet already you have become disobedient. I see you need to be taught a lesson when I get you home."

Did he really think of the house where he had kept her prisoner as her home?

Given his obsession with fables, she supposed he was delusional enough to somehow believe that she was a willing participant in his games.

"That's it, Grace. I've had enough. Either you come out before I count to three or I shoot poor Barbara in the foot. One."

No surely he wouldn't.

"Two."

She almost moved but forced herself to stay still, positive Emmanuel wouldn't follow through with the threat.

"Three. Remember, Grace, this is your fault. She's about to suffer because of you."

The sound of the gunshot seemed exorbitantly loud in the quiet night.

Barbara grunted in pain, screaming through the gag, and Grace's stomach heaved.

He'd done it.

He'd shot her.

"Come, Grace. Now. Unless you wish me to shoot her other foot? A hand perhaps? Or a knee?"

There was no way she could stay here and not do anything to stop him from hurting the other woman. Elijah knew she was a few streets over, but she hadn't been paying attention to the street they were on so she hadn't been able to give him a name. Without her exact location it could still be several more minutes before he got here. Plenty of time for Emmanuel to inflict more pain.

"I'm aiming for her shoulder this time, Grace, and you only have until I count to two to get out here, I'm losing patience. When I finish with her, I'm going to go back to the car and make sure your shadow is finished off. Did he force himself on you, Grace, like the last male friend you had?"

How did he know that?

There were only two people she had told that she'd been raped and one of them was bleeding out in the car.

She began to tremble as she realized who Emmanuel really was.

"One."

Even though she knew this was a bad idea, Grace felt backed into a corner. All she could do was pray that the cops showed up before Emmanuel disappeared with her because there was no way she was hiding while Barbara was shot over and over again."

"Two."

"No, wait," she called out as she scrambled from under the bush. "I'm coming, please don't hurt her."

Keeping the cell phone in her pocket with the hopes that even if Emmanuel did take off with her, she could be tracked through the phone's GPS, she walked toward her tormentor with her hands held up in surrender.

"There's my good girl," he said, speaking to her as though she were his pet and not a person. But to him she wasn't a person, not really, she was a prop in his own sick, demented game.

"Why are you doing this?" she asked, hoping to stall him a little. She only needed to buy a small amount of time.

"Now is not the time for twenty questions. If I'm not mistaken your posse will be here any moment." Without another word, he aimed the gun at Barbara Lack and fired, hitting the poor woman in the head.

Grace stared in shock for a second.

She hadn't expected him to do that.

"Why?" she asked as tears trickled down her cheeks.

Instead of answering her, Emmanuel stepped closer, pulled his hood back so she could see his face and gave her a smile that had her blood running cold.

She turned to run, knowing she had made a mistake in showing herself, but it was too late.

Something slammed into the back of her head and the world dissolved into nothingness around her.

~

2:33 P.M.

Matthew felt like he was stuck in mud.

Thick, gloopy mud that covered every inch of his body, weighing him down, making it difficult to move. To think.

Slowly, sensations began to filter into his consciousness.

The soft beep of a machine.

The strong smell of antiseptic.

The hovering presence beside him.

And pain.

A lot of pain.

Images flipped through his mind, hovering there only long enough for him to get a glimpse before another picture took its place.

Blonde curls against his shoulder.

The alert of a cell phone.

A car.

Shattering glass.

Searing pain.

Tears.

Pain of a different kind.

This pain was loss, the deep sense of knowing you weren't going to get to have what was most precious to you.

Grace.

The thought came screaming into his mind with an intensity that nudged his brain out of the mud and back into reality.

The second safehouse had been compromised, he'd tried to get her away, to the precinct where she would be safe. They'd been in the car when Emmanuel had shot him and he'd lost control, causing them to crash.

He'd thought he was dying, been terrified to leave Grace alone and unprotected.

Emmanuel would come for her.

The man was insane but determined.

He had to warn the others, tell them ... something. Something important. A thought hovered just out of reach. He knew it would break this case wide open, finally get them ahead instead of constantly running behind Emmanuel waiting for him to mess up.

Matthew tried to open his eyes, sit up, speak, but found his body was completely uncooperative.

"Looks like he's waking up."

The voice sounded like it was underwater and a thousand miles away, but he heard it, and recognized it.

It sounded like one of Grace's brothers, he couldn't tell which, Elijah and Jeremiah were identical twins and hard to tell apart, something that would change as he got to know them better because there was no way he was walking away from Grace, not for anything. But that meant he had to get his body to cooperate, had to wake up, had to figure out what he knew.

Grace's life depended on it, of that he felt certain.

"Matthew? Can you hear me?"

Yes.

The word echoed inside his head, but he was pretty sure it didn't make it out of his mind.

"Matthew, you need to wake up. Grace needs you. He has her."

Fear crawled over his skin like a million spiders.

Emmanuel had Grace.

He dragged in a breath, welcoming the shooting pains emanating from his chest because it meant he was alive, it meant he could still fight for Grace.

He just had to fight against his own body first.

"Come on, Matthew, wake up."

The last was delivered as an order, and he allowed it to give him the last push he needed.

His eyes opened but everything was blurry, shades of gray, and nothing made sense.

He blinked to try to clear his vision, and it worked because when a face leaned over him, he could see that it was whichever of Grace's brothers had been talking to him.

"You with me?" the other man asked.

"Yeah," Matthew croaked.

"Here."

A straw was held to his lips, and he sipped the cool liquid. It refreshed not just his throat but rejuvenated his body as well. He could feel the cobwebs washing away, his strength returning. "You said he has Grace."

"Elijah, he awake yet?" Allina asked, entering the hospital room.

"Just woke up," Elijah replied.

"Do you have news on Grace?" Matthew asked, judging his returning strength and whether or not he was ready to get out of here.

Who was he kidding?

He was leaving here as soon as he found out what was going on. No way was he sitting in a hospital bed while Grace was out there somewhere fighting for her life.

"Nothing new. We were hoping you would be able to tell us something," Ali replied. Her blue eyes were red-rimmed, it was clear she'd been crying earlier—probably the whole Bennett family had been. How were they going to cope if Grace didn't come home?

They had just gotten her back after five and a half years of searching. She'd been doing better than anyone could have hoped even though her struggles were far from over, and now, just like that, she was gone again.

This time they might not find her.

Emmanuel might have taken her far away or hidden her someplace where they wouldn't be able to find her. Or he could have killed her.

Things had changed. Emmanuel's games had been exposed, there was every chance he had changed his plans. Just because he couldn't let

Grace go didn't mean he was going to let her live. A murder suicide was a definite possibility.

"Matthew?"

He blinked, realized he'd zoned out, and forced himself to focus.

Grace was counting on him.

"How did he get her? I told her to run, get help." Which she'd obviously done since he was still alive. An ambulance must have reached him before he bled out, and although there was pain in his chest, he felt better than he thought he probably should. No doubt the adrenalin rush of learning Grace had been taken again.

"He didn't come alone. He brought Barbara Lack with him. The woman had a bullet wound in her foot and had been killed with a single bullet to the head," Elijah explained.

"He kidnapped her to use as bait, in case he needed motivation to get Grace to come to him," he said.

"It worked," Allina said.

Elijah swore then raked his fingers through his hair. "I was on the phone with her. I told her I was coming, that we'd be there soon. It only took us eleven minutes to get to her from when she phoned, we probably missed her by only a minute or two. A minute or two," he repeated, anger and grief mingled together on his face.

That same memory that had teased him while he was regaining consciousness poked at him now.

There was something important he had to remember.

The key.

He knew it was and yet he couldn't force the hazy memory to clear.

"If he didn't get her then he would have gotten her some other time, he was determined," Allina reminded her husband as she slipped her arms around his waist.

"Did you hear something? See something?" Elijah asked, desperation in his voice.

"There's something," he said, frustrated with himself. What did he know?

Elijah's eyes lit up. "Come on, man, figure it out, my sister is counting on you."

"You think I don't know that?" he snapped. "You think I'm not trying to figure it out?"

"Getting angry isn't going to help you," Ali said, playing peacemaker. "Try to calm down. You were weak, you lost a lot of blood. Bullet got you in the chest, but it was low and bounced off your ribs, missing everything important, it went through and through. He wasn't trying to kill you, just get you out of the way. You would have been tired, but you were still looking out for Grace, you told her to run, to get someplace safe knowing he'd be coming. You were unconscious by the time we got to you, but you might have only just passed out. Emmanuel shot the woman, using a different weapon, not the sniper rifle. You would have heard it, it might have roused you. Try to put yourself back in the car, what did you hear?"

Clearing everything else from his mind he focused.

He'd been tired, struggling to keep his eyes open, listening for signs of help coming.

He'd been drifting off when he heard the gunshot.

Then a man's voice.

I'm aiming for her shoulder this time, Grace, and you only have until I count to two to get out here, I'm losing patience. When I finish with her, I'm going to go back to the car and make sure your shadow is finished off. Did he force himself on you, Grace, like the last male friend you had?

The words echoed inside his head as his gaze snapped up. "I know who he is." Matthew began removing the tubes and wires attached to his body. He needed clothes and shoes so he could get out of here.

"What are you doing?" Elijah demanded. "And what do you mean you know who he is?"

"I don't think they're discharging you," Allina added.

"Don't care, I'm not sitting around here while that maniac has Grace."

"Who is he?" Elijah asked.

"I don't know his name," he said as he threw back the covers. "But Grace was raped at a party two months before she was taken. She was drugged and assaulted by someone she knew, but was ashamed, thought no one would believe her, so she didn't say anything. By the time she realized she wanted to, she tried calling Jeremiah, but he was on a case, and she just left a message for him to call her. Then she called a sexual assault helpline and spoke to someone. The only people who know what happened to her are me and whoever she spoke to that day. That's the connection, it has to be. We need to talk with the families of the other victims, see if any of them were sexually assaulted. And we need to get a list of everyone who works at the helpline because one of them is Emmanuel."

~

3:58 P.M.

Her head was fuzzy.

That horrible kind of cottony feeling that came with being drugged.

Grace moaned as memories poured into her mind too fast, making her head throb to a painful beat, in time with her pulse that felt like it was thumping far too fast.

She remembered everything, the shooting, the car crash, Emmanuel shooting Barbara Lack, and allowing herself to be taken.

After that, her memories ceased. She knew that Emmanuel had hit her over the head to knock her out, but he must have also given her something to make sure she stayed asleep until he had her where he wanted her.

Which he now did.

Once again, she was his helpless victim.

Anger coursed through her, setting her alight, shoving away the lingering fuzziness from the sedatives, and making her burn with a fury she hadn't felt before. Of course, she had been angry when Emmanuel had abducted her the first time, but she had been much younger then, a lot more naïve, and she hadn't had as much to live for as she did today.

Today she had *everything* to live for.

Matthew.

The man had saved her life when he and his partner stumbled by accident on Emmanuel's house of horrors, but he had also saved her soul. She honestly wasn't sure if she would be anything but a sobbing, hysterical basket case if it wasn't for him. Her family meant everything to her, but they didn't understand what it was like to take a life when it wasn't something you had to do as part of your job. That simple understanding from Matthew because of what he'd gone through with his stepfather had opened up her heart to him. He'd given her a gift he hadn't even realized when he'd trusted her with his pain, and in doing so had earned her trust.

Now Emmanuel might have killed the man she was falling in love with, and she wanted to kill him for it.

Fear left her.

What good was being afraid of dying when she was just as afraid to live without Matthew in her life?

Now she'd rather stand tall and fight to the death, even if killing Emmanuel meant she would die too.

No more fear.

Anger.

She needed to hold onto her anger, cling to it if she had to, so she could do what needed to be done.

"I know you're awake, my angel." Emmanuel's voice was accompanied by the touch of his hand gliding down her back.

Her bare back.

He'd stripped her clothes off.

Grace wasn't quite sure why she was surprised, it was a typical Emmanuel move. He knew how to make her feel her most vulnerable and he delighted in doing it. Those first few months she had spent with him he'd kept her naked almost constantly. He'd wanted to manipulate her, beat her down so she had no choice but to comply with his orders if she wanted to survive. Eventually, she had learned that doing as he demanded was easier than fighting against him, and once she realized that, her life had been easier. Clothes, nicer food, hot water, more choices for things to do to pass away the long and lonely hours she spent locked in her room.

"Everything is going to be okay, we're together again now," he said as his hand moved to stroke her hair.

Forcing herself not to give in to the sick feeling in her stomach from his touch, she tried to take in as much as she could of her surroundings.

She was on her stomach on something soft, likely a bed. When she tried to move, she found that all of her limbs were tied down.

She knew what that meant.

Emmanuel was ready to punish her.

Still, she wasn't going to complain. All she had to do was stay alive. There was no way that her family wasn't going to go all out to find her. This time they knew that Emmanuel was obsessed with her. Surely, they would figure out that she knew who he was. If Matthew was alive then maybe he'd tell them about her rape, and if he did, they'd have to figure out the link, surely.

"You know why I have to do this, don't you, angel?" he asked as he took hold of her chin and turned her head so it was facing him. Even though her eyes were still closed she could perfectly picture his face in her head.

There was no point in giving an answer, no matter what she said it would be wrong. That was a lesson she had learned long ago.

"It pains me as much as it pains you," he murmured before she heard the familiar sound of the whip slicing through the air.

It cut into the flesh on her back with a bite that felt like it was trying to eat her alive.

She managed not to cry out for the first few strikes.

"I know who you are," she said when she started to feel wetness on her back and knew he had broken the skin enough she was bleeding.

"Of course you do, we have spent many years together."

"No, I mean I know that I knew you before. You were the man on the line at the rape crisis hotline. I told you what happened to me. You were the first one I confessed to. Why did you do this to me when you knew what I had already been through? Were the others all victims too? Is that why you chose us? Why do you hate rape victims?"

"Hate rape victims?" he echoed.

There was something in his voice that had her opening her eyes to find that he was standing, whip still in hand, staring at her as though she had just grown three extra heads. She had always been interested in psychology, in the way the mind worked, what led people to become the person they were. That fascination was what had led her to decide to follow in Jem's footsteps and work as a criminal psychologist. There was always a reason why killers did what they did.

Always.

Maybe she had just stumbled upon Emmanuel's reasons.

"Then tell me why, please," she asked softly.

Emmanuel dropped the whip and stalked around the room, dragging his fingers through his hair. It was clear he was agitated, but she didn't know if that was going to work for or against her.

Something was different about Emmanuel, a twitchiness that said he wasn't the same man she remembered. Before Emmanuel had been calm, always in control. He might get angry with her when she didn't do what he wanted her to do, but the rest of the time he was always infuriatingly calm.

Now he was anything but.

"I'm trying to help you," Emmanuel said, with such sincerity that she believed he believed that. "I didn't want you to hurt yourselves like she did."

Keeping her tone soothing, Grace asked, "Like who?"

"My sister." His voice was tortured, and pain was written all over his face.

"She was raped?"

"She was only fourteen. She was my big sister, I was eight, and I idolized her. I tried to help, I tried to make her smile again, but she was so sad. I didn't understand. I didn't know what sex was let alone rape. I tried to help her, but it didn't work, she took her own life. Everything fell apart after that."

"You started working at the rape crisis line to help victims like me because you couldn't help your sister."

"It wasn't enough. I had to do more. I wanted you to grow strong, so you didn't give in like my sister did to the pain those men put inside you. My sister ... I loved her ... but she wasn't strong. She let that pain destroy her and once she was gone my dad just stopped living, gave up, mom got angry, started drinking, hitting ..."

"She abused you," Grace finished for him. It all made sense now, Emmanuel as a small boy, had seen something horrific happen to his sister even if he didn't quite understand it. Tried to help her but failed when she ended her own life. Then the dad fell into a grief fueled depression, and the mom became an abusive drunk. He wanted to save other rape victims because he hadn't saved his sister. In his mind his sister had been weak, he wanted to make other victims strong. She had no idea where the fable thing came into it, but he'd obviously decided it was his job to help rape victims find their strength.

"She was destroyed by the man who raped her daughter," Emmanuel said. "I didn't want anyone else to be destroyed by that same violence. I made you strong, Grace. Me. I didn't let it destroy you. I wouldn't. I knew the moment I heard your voice that I had to save you." He moved closer to the bed, ran his fingers through the blood on her back and held up his hand for her to see. "That's why I did this, it's why you had to bleed, to fight, you had to be strong. I couldn't lose you too. I couldn't lose you too," he repeated, tears shimmering in his eyes.

"Emmanuel," she said gently, knowing she was only going to have one chance at convincing him that he had to let her go. "I understand, I do, but it doesn't have to be this way. You were strong for me, you didn't let my rape destroy me, you helped me grow strong, now let me do the same for you. Let me save you."

∼

5:03 P.M.

Matthew grunted as he shifted in his seat.

The wound on his chest was bandaged, and he really was very lucky. It was clear that Emmanuel hadn't been trying to kill either him, or any of the other cops who had been watching the safehouse. The man had started shooting, injured a couple, but there were no fatalities other than Barbara Lack.

"The rape crisis line is still dragging their heels getting us a list of names," Elijah announced, frustration heavy in his tone.

"Did you tell them one of their counsellors has been using the crisis line to hunt victims and abduct and murder them?" he growled. What were they thinking? It was one thing to say they wouldn't hand out a list of names without a court order because they didn't want to breach the volunteers' confidentiality, but one of those men was a killer. There was zero doubt about that. If Emmanuel was the man who had raped Grace or one of the men who held her down that night, she would have said that. The only other person besides himself who knew was the counsellor she'd spoken to.

"They said there's no proof," Elijah said.

He slammed his fist into the desk. "No proof? Grace only told two people that she'd been raped, me and the counselor at the crisis line. The man who shot Barbara Lack and took Grace knew that she'd been raped. And we know that at least half a dozen of the other victims had been sexually assaulted, meaning it's a good chance they also called the crisis line. What more proof do they need?" After he'd shared what he remembered, they'd started contacting families to see if this was indeed the link, and while they still had several more to check with, of the ten families they'd asked, six of them had confirmed that prior to going missing their daughters, wives, and sisters had been victims of rape.

"Forensics, I guess," Elijah said, wearily rubbing at the back of his neck.

"Well, we'd have forensics if they'd give us a list of names." He huffed. CSU tech Kane Curtis had an abundance of fingerprints and DNA evidence, he just had nothing to compare them to. Which if they could get a list of all past and present counselors, they'd be able to ask for samples. Most people would be happy to volunteer their prints and DNA to clear themselves and help a dangerous man get locked away. Those that didn't even if they couldn't compel a judge to force them to provide samples, they'd at least have a small list of suspects to work through.

"We'll have to focus on what we do have," Rylla said.

Matthew looked at his partner with what he knew was close to hopelessness. Everyone had gathered at the station when they learned Grace had been taken again. He appreciated everyone's support, appreciated that they were all rallying around him and the Bennett family, but what good was it if they couldn't find her?

"You figured that this guy might have building experience given the things he built in the basement of Mable White's house," Jonathon said.

"And that he already knew Natalie Potter before he killed her," Nickolas Sleigh, a fellow detective who was married to Jonathon's wife's sister Agape, said thoughtfully.

"We went through her neighbors and none of them were builders or worked in the industry," Rylla told them.

"Did you talk to all the neighbors or just look at who owned the houses?" Rylla's husband Nate asked.

"We were able to speak to a few of the neighbors in person, but the rest we cross referenced who owned the houses with a list of builders," Rylla replied. "Of course, it's not a comprehensive list and we know that Emmanuel might be living in someone else's house, but so far, all the owners of the houses have been accounted for. There's a chance that while he might have known Natalie, or at least seen her around before, that he's not a neighbor. Or we could be completely wrong about the whole thing and he did just randomly cross paths with her that day."

"I don't think so," Matthew said slowly, picking up the list of Natalie's neighbors.

"What are you thinking?" Naomi Zeeke asked. She and her husband Sam were Jonathon's in-laws. She was also Rylla's best friend, and she and her husband, while not cops, were experienced and had volunteered to help however they could.

"That maybe we found Emmanuel's real home," he said. There was one name on the list that kept standing out to him. "The house directly across the street from Natalie's is owned by an older woman, she and her family have lived in the house for the last four decades, she has a son who's in his early thirties."

"You think the son could be Emmanuel?" Sam Zeeke asked.

"I think it's a possibility. We need to find out everything we can about that family." There was something in his gut that said they needed to look into this man. Jason Yamagada. An innocuous looking man who could fit the sketch Grace had given of the man who had tormented her.

"Jason Yamagada owns a business flipping houses," Allina said, reading off her laptop. "From what I can find he had a sister, Isabel who committed suicide when she was fifteen, Jason was nine at the time. After that, the father became depressed, his business almost went bankrupt, looks like they almost lost the house but managed to hold onto it. Mrs. Yamagada has a whole bunch of DUIs."

"She turned to alcohol, her husband turned to anti-depressants, what happened to poor little Jason?" Allayna asked.

"That." Matthew pointed to the whiteboard at the end of the room where pictures of all of Emmanuel's victims, along with Grace, were pinned. "That's what happened to him. Why did the sister commit suicide?"

Ali tapped away at her computer, her eyes widening as she looked back at them all. "Isabel was raped."

"That's the link," he said, a rush of adrenalin masking the stubborn pain in his side. While he was lucky the bullet hadn't done more damage, he had lost a lot of blood, and he was still a little woozy, but nothing was keeping him in a hospital bed while Grace was out there waiting for him to find her. "Jason volunteered at the rape crisis line because of what happened to his sister. Because his sister committed suicide and his family fell apart, he decided he was going to play God and try to make other rape victims strong. His version of strong anyway. That has to be why he had that obsession with the fable games. His way of trying to make them strong so they wouldn't end their lives."

"He did it for them," Jeremiah added bitterly. Matthew knew the fact that Grace had reached out to him after her assault to tell him about it and he hadn't replied because he'd been busy on a case was eating at the older man. But there was no way that Jeremiah could have known what Grace wanted to talk about, and she'd given him no reason to believe it was urgent.

None of that mattered right now though.

All that mattered was getting Grace back alive.

"Call the crisis line back, tell them we have a name and all we need is confirmation that he works there," he told Elijah.

While the other man picked the phone back up, and the others began to talk quietly amongst themselves, Matthew's mind wandered to Grace.

Where was she right now?

Was she hurt?

Did she think he was dead?

Did she know that he would move heaven and earth to find her?

Hold on, sweetheart, he begged, throwing the words out into the Universe and praying that somehow they found their way to Grace.

The thought of her being trapped, bound, imprisoned all over again made bile burn his throat as it threatened to come exploding out.

How was he going to cope if they didn't find Grace?

Or if they found her too late?

"We got him," Elijah announced gleefully, a flicker of hope in his blue eyes.

Matthew felt that same hope spring to life inside him. "Jason was a volunteer there?"

"For the last decade," Elijah confirmed.

"We need to get to his mother's house," he said already shoving back from the table, wincing as the stitches in his side pulled.

"You need to stay here, you're in no condition to go anywhere unless it's right back to the hospital," Jeremiah said, stopping him with a hand to the shoulder.

He brushed the hand aside and met the other man's stare, then met the gaze of every other person in the room. "No one is stopping me from going after Grace. I was the one with her when he got her, I'm the one who failed her, I'm the one who promised her that I'd keep her safe, and I'm the one who's falling in love with her. Nothing, not a single one of you, is going to stop me from going after my girl and killing the man who hurt her."

5:11 P.M.

Emmanuel, or Jason as he had just confessed his real name to her, was pacing around the room in a near frenetic manner.

The pacing was making her head spin. It still pounded with a headache, no doubt a mixture of hitting it when the car crashed earlier and the drugs that Jason had given her. Grace's whole body ached like she was one giant bruise, and the wounds on her back stung with a ferocity she had allowed herself to forget. What she wanted was to soak in a nice hot bath, allowing the water to soothe her aching muscles. Then she wanted to curl up in Matthew's arms and go to sleep feeling safe and protected.

But there was no Matthew here to soothe her.

For all she knew, she would never feel the warmth of his touch, the gentle caress of his fingers, or the softness of his lips against hers.

Anger threatened to take over again, but she shoved it away. Jason was unbalanced, he truly believed he was helping her by making her strong with all his tests and games. Getting angry with him wouldn't work, but she prayed she could talk him into letting her go.

"Jason, thank you for everything that you've done for me, because of you, I *have* grown strong, and I *have* survived my assault, but now it's time for me to help you," she said patiently.

"Help me?" he asked, pausing on her other side so she had to turn her head to see him. Grace hated being this vulnerable to him, lying on her stomach, her arms and legs bound, naked and exposed, injured and hurting, but she had to make the best of what she had.

"I think you deserve it, don't you?"

"I deserve it?" His brow crinkled and she saw a glimpse of the terrified boy he must have been, losing his sister, and then having his mother take out her grief in alcohol fueled violence while his father gave into depression. It didn't make it okay what he had done to her or all those other women, but it did help her to understand.

"Of course you do. Why don't you untie me, and I promise you that I'll get you the help you need. It's time, Jason."

That seemed to snap him into some sort of trance, and he nodded slowly. "It's time," he intoned the blankness in his voice scaring her.

"Yes, time to go."

"You're right." He snapped into action as though propelled by a force she didn't understand.

Her heart raced when she saw him move away and then return with a knife. Was this it? Was he going to kill her? "Jason?"

"Don't worry, my sweet angel, you were right. It's time."

An almost maniacal smile lit his lips, and she knew whatever he had planned next wasn't good. He cut the rope at her wrists first, where the rope was tied around the bedpost, turning her awkwardly over as much as he could with her ankles still bound, then tied the two ends of the rope together, binding her wrists once more.

Only then did he free her legs and drag her off the bed. "Jason, where are we going?" Grace asked as he led her out of the bedroom and into a hall.

"To find peace," he murmured, and she had a feeling she was definitely not going to like his idea of peace.

"I've found peace already, Jason," she implored as he pulled her down a flight of stairs. "With the man who's been staying with me in the safehouses. He's a good man, and I think he's falling in love with me, I know I'm falling in love with him. I've found my peace, please, Jason, let me help you find yours."

Jason paused, palmed her cheek, then leaned down and touched a kiss to her forehead. "You have helped me, my angel. And now it is time to set you free. For us both to be free."

Yeah, she was totally not liking the sound of that.

Jason pulled her along with him through a hall, then a large open plan kitchen, dining, living room, and finally outside.

Immediately she grabbed hold of her opportunity, there might not be another one. "Help!" Grace screamed at the top of her lungs. "Someone please, help me!"

"Stop," Jason demanded, slamming his fist into the side of her head hard enough that she saw stars.

Her knees buckled, she would have hit the ground if he hadn't picked her up first and slung her over his shoulder, carrying her with him down to the back of the garden.

She tried to fight.

Tried to shove away from him.

But the world kept spinning around her in a series of sickening revolutions that almost had her throwing up.

Then she was falling.

It felt like she dropped hundreds of feet, but really it couldn't be more than four or five.

She landed with a thud that forced the air from her lungs.

A face hovered above her and she blinked to try to clear away the blurriness. "Please," she begged, "please let me go."

"I am, angel. I'm finally setting you free." Jason assured her with such conviction that she knew he had lost whatever touch with reality he'd still had.

With a horrifying air of finality, something slammed down above her blocking her view of Jason and the bright blue sky behind him.

It took a moment for reality to break through the denial she was trying to cling to.

A coffin.

Jason had just thrown her into a coffin and closed the lid.

She could hear small thumps, rhythmically spaced, and knew they were him throwing dirt down into the hole.

Burying her alive.

"No!" she screamed, banging her bound hands on the lid of the coffin, trying to shift it. It moved a little, and for a second Grace thought she actually stood a chance at getting out of here.

But the dirt kept coming with surprising speed, weighing down the lid, making it impossible to move again.

Hysteria welled up inside her, bubbling out in a throat burning scream as she hammered frantically at the coffin lid, trying to break through it with nothing but her fingernails, her fists, and pure determination.

"Jason! Don't do this. Please," the last was said on a sob as she began to cry. Huge, chest heaving wails that stole her ability to breathe.

She was going to die.

Even if Matthew lived and he'd been conscious and managed to hear what Jason had said and put the pieces together and figured out he was the man at the rape crisis line she'd spoken to. And even if they managed to find out Jason's name, and then figure out where he was living, he'd still have to figure out that Jason had buried her alive in a coffin that would soon become her tome.

And all within around five hours or so.

Much less if she couldn't get her emotions under control.

The calmer she was, the slower she would use up the precious supply of oxygen that she had left.

"Come on, Grace, calm down, stop crying," she begged herself through the tears that refused to stop falling. "For Matthew."

If he was alive, she couldn't let him spend the rest of his life carrying around the guilt of her death.

He would, she knew that.

Just as she carried the guilt of the women whose lives Jason had forced her to take, he carried the guilt of the death of his stepfather and the shame his mother and sister had heaped upon him. He'd carry her death too, and she was so afraid that the added burden would be enough to squash the light inside him.

That light had led her out of the darkness. It had given her hope and a promise of a future where the ties to her dark past had only minimal hold on her life.

There was no way she could be responsible for blowing that light out.

So, she had to calm down, had to at least give Matthew and her family the best chance possible of finding her. That was the only way she might find peace in whatever lay beyond this earth.

There had been many times when she had been Jason's prisoner that she had prayed for just one more minute with her family. A chance to hug them one last time, tell them how much she loved them, how lucky she felt to have been born into a family—both blood and by choice—that loved each other so much.

She had gotten an answer to that prayer.

A chance to spend time with her family and so very much more.

The last few days had been both awful and beautiful. She had battled the desire to give in to the pain and fear and let it consume her, and begun to forge a new path, one where she could make a difference in the world and one where she had found true companionship.

If this was the end, then she had to focus on the gifts she'd been given and not everything Jason had stolen from her. While she could never be grateful to Jason for what he'd done, even if it had made her stronger, shown her her ability to survive, it had at least set her on a path to find Matthew.

When the oxygen ran out and death finally got its claws in her, it would be Matthew's smiling face she would cling to as she stepped over the divide to what lay beyond.

~

6:26 P.M.

Jason put the last shovel full of dirt into the hole.

There.

It was done.

He patted the dirt down with the back of the shovel and then looked around. He wasn't sure what to do next. Maybe he should throw some of the grass seed from the shed over the top of the soil, or perhaps he should plant something special like roses. A memorial of sorts.

When he'd taken Grace, he'd assumed that he would pick things back up right from where they had left off. The house was set up just like the one before and he'd intended to punish Grace for leaving him just like his sister had, and then he was going to let things calm down before he took another woman.

Things had changed when Grace had offered him her help.

How long had it been since someone noticed him enough to offer him anything?

His sister hadn't loved him enough to fight through what had happened to her and live. His mother hadn't loved him enough to remember that she still had a child alive, and a child who needed her. His father hadn't loved him enough to fight his way through the fog of grief and stop his wife's alcohol fueled abuse.

Things had gotten so bad at home that he had withdrawn at school and the friends he'd had before faded from his life. Since he was quiet and didn't cause disruptions in class, teachers basically ignored him. After graduating high school, he'd taken over his father's construction company, managing to repair the damage his father's apathy had caused the business. He was successful, he still took care of his parents despite their abandonment. He had volunteered at the rape crisis line because he didn't want another woman to feel she had no options but to end her own life, destroying the family members she left behind.

But it wasn't enough.

He'd failed Isabel, and he hadn't been enough to save his parents, but he had made a difference.

What he'd done for Grace proved that.

And now it was time to move on.

Grace had given him exactly what he needed. She'd seen him. *Really* seen him. Understood what he'd gone through, the pain of loss after loss after loss.

She was his angel.

His bright, beautiful, strong angel.

And it was time for her to gain her wings.

Time for him to gain his wings as well because he was the one responsible for saving Grace. Without him, she would have withered away into nothingness. Her rape would have destroyed her, he knew it the moment he heard her voice on the phone. But his games had helped her. The book of fables he'd read each night when he crept into Isabel's room trying to calm her tears hadn't helped his sister, but it had helped Grace.

Saved her.

Turned her into his angel.

Now they were both free.

Free to face eternity together.

Jason hoped they found his sister when they passed on. Had she become an angel or had her taking her own life sent her straight to the Devil's playground?

As much as he hoped he would be reunited with Isabel, so long as he had his angel Grace then he would be happy. His sweet, beautiful girl, he couldn't wait to hold her again. Only this time it would be different, this time he wouldn't have to be her teacher, she had already found her inner strength. This time they would be able to just be together.

He couldn't wait.

Brushing the dirt from his hands, Jason set the shovel aside, resting it against one of the large trees standing guard on either side of Grace's grave. It seemed only fitting that he do something special to mark this spot, his angel's final resting place before she gained her wings.

While he wouldn't be able to keep coming back here to visit—there would be no need to, they would both be together in the afterlife—he still wanted this place to be special.

A beautiful water feature. Perhaps an angel.

Yes, that would be perfect.

Jason took a look at his watch. Grace had probably five hours which should be more than enough time for him to take a quick shower, hop in his car, drive to the local garden nursery and find an appropriate water feature. Then all he had to do was bring it back, set it up out here, and then it was time.

There was no fear in him, he was ready for death.

For so long he had thought it was something to fear, but it had given Isabel a peace that nothing else—not him, nor their parents—had been able to give her. In fact, to her it had been the only thing that could provide her what she needed. Before Isabel's suicide, he had thought death was a lonely thing. He'd thought you were all alone, but one night just days before Isabel's death he'd been in her room and they'd talked. Jason had crept into her room most nights after her weeping woke him, and Isabel had told him that death wasn't lonely it was the opposite.

It was never being alone again.

It was calm, soothing, peaceful, like sitting beside a stream on a warm summer evening. Fireflies were just starting to come out, the odd lazy cloud crept across the sky, the gentle sound of water tumbling over the rocks mixed with the sounds of crickets.

That was what death was like.

It was like forever being in that beautiful spot, surrounded by nature, only the best part was that the people you loved were there too.

Soon he and Grace would never have to worry about anyone coming between them again. No one would be sneaking into their home to steal her away from him. He was tying them together in the only way he knew that couldn't be undone. He was joining them in death.

Once Grace's memorial was finished it was his time to pass on.

With a smile on his face, he headed inside. He took a long drink of water, it was hot work digging, especially in the summer heat. Then he headed upstairs to his bathroom. Despite the dirt smudging his cheeks, and the sweat dotted on his forehead, he looked happy. There was a peace in his eyes that hadn't been there ever since the day of Isabel's rape.

Jason still remembered that day. It was etched into his mind, his dad had taken him for another shooting lesson, and then they'd been tossing a football in the front yard, then the call had come in, Isabel had been hurt. They'd all rushed to the hospital, there had been no sitter to watch him, so his parents had taken him along. He had crept away while his parents were talking with the cops, he'd wanted to find his big sister, cheer her up like he always did when she was crying over some boy. Instead, he found her in a hospital gown, on a gurney, sobbing, her legs spread as a doctor worked between them.

He hadn't understood then what was going on, but now he knew they were doing the rape kit.

That moment had stuck with him ever since.

How could a man hurt a woman like that?

Women were beautiful creatures, meant to be cherished.

That's what he'd do for his sweet angel. He would make sure Grace had the most beautiful memorial, something that represented her personality, then once they both gained their wings, she would spend eternity knowing how much he loved her.

For nine long years he had lived in his parents' home, enduring the beatings and his mother's screams, his father's silence and blank stares, even while being in the room while Jason was being hit by his mother, and through all of it he had been alone. He'd left as soon as he could, but the loneliness hadn't gone away. There had been girlfriends but none of them were right, they didn't really see him, didn't understand him.

Then there was Grace.

Jason had known the moment he heard her voice that she was special. Had known she was different the night he'd entered her home and taken her with him. Had known she was strong when she had survived every lesson he taught, learned everything he wanted her too, and aced every test.

When he was with her, he wasn't alone, he wasn't anyone's punching bag, and he wasn't a failure.

There was no way he could go on without her. Grace was his redemption.

～

9:55 P.M.

Matthew prayed they were right about this because he had a sickening feeling in his gut that said Grace was quickly running out of time.

After they'd gotten Jason Yamagada's name, they'd gone to his parents' house, where they learned that their son had been there the day of the abduction attempt at the hospital, the day Natalie Potter had been killed. He'd been right when he thought that Emmanuel had to have already known Natalie, but because the house was his parents, and Jason had his own place, they hadn't been able to connect him right away.

Once they knew they had their man it should have been simple enough to end this. Go to Jason's house, arrest him, rescue Grace, they all lived happily ever after, the end.

Only it hadn't turned out that simple.

After their daughter's suicide, Mr. Yamagada had allowed his construction company to all but fall apart. Upon graduating, Jason had taken over, managing to rebuild the business into something much more profitable than it had been before. But the way he had done that was to move from construction to house flipping. Besides the apartment he lived in, Jason was currently the owner of six properties that he was in the process of renovating and flipping.

That made seven properties that had to be checked.

Of course, they'd gone to the apartment first since it was the place where he actually resided, but they'd known before they got there that it wouldn't be where he would go with a kidnap victim in tow.

He'd need more privacy which meant they were now checking out the other properties. They'd split up to cover more ground, but the properties were spread far and wide across the city, and it took time to get to each one of them and clear them. Checking for signs as to whether Jason had spent any time there other than working on them with his teams.

So far, they had eliminated three of the buildings, but that still left three of them to go.

He, Elijah, Allina, and Jonathon had just pulled up outside property number five. It was a pretty-looking house that looked like it was already finished, or close to it. There was a stone fence that had vines growing over it, the front door was framed by a cute little porch also covered in vines, only this vine was a mass of pink flowers. There were dormer windows on the third floor, bright white shutters on the first two floors' windows, and the door had been painted a bright, cheery yellow. The garden consisted of two large trees and flowerbeds framing the front of the house. It was a beautiful property, and he could see why Jason had made such a success of the business after taking over from his father. He did great work, paid attention to detail, and didn't just present a finished house but a dream of a future where you could all but hear children laughing, and see them playing, swinging from branch to branch in the trees, and chasing each other across the lawn.

It was a future he wanted with Grace, one he was determined to have which meant he had to find her.

The four of them climbed out of the car, and he winced as the wound on his chest protested yet another movement when all it wanted to do was lie still.

"You okay?" Allina asked.

"Fine," he gritted out. Matthew was getting sick and tired of being asked that question. Whether he was all right or not, Grace was in a much more serious position, and he wasn't resting until he could do so with her tucked safely in his arms.

"I think we should take you back to the hospital after we check out this place," Elijah said. "Jem, Laynie, Sam, and Naomi are at the sixth house, and Nick, Nate, and Rylla are at the seventh. If he's not at any of them then he's set himself up at a property not in his name, like he did with Mable White. If he's done that, we're not going to catch him tonight. You may as well rest."

"No." If they didn't find Grace at one of Jason's houses then there was a very good chance that they wouldn't find her.

Ever.

They couldn't go knocking on every door in the city, not that he wouldn't do just that, but there was no way that his bosses would okay that.

"I don't need rest, I need Grace," he said.

"We all want to find her," Elijah said.

"Trust me, no one wants to find her more than I do," he said. While Grace's family might have loved her longer, nobody could love her more than he did. She was his future, his salvation, his chance at a redemption many would say he didn't need but that he was determined to find.

"We're the ones who—"

"Guys, arguing isn't helping, we need to keep the focus on Grace," Allina cut her husband off, doing her best to placate both of them, but emotions were running too high for all of them right now.

"Roof," Jonathon said, the one word capturing all of their attention.

"What?" Matthew asked.

"I see someone on the roof," Jonathon elaborated.

They all turned their attention toward the house and Matthew saw exactly what had caught Jonathon's attention. There was a shadowy figure moving on the roof, and immediately he knew it was Jason.

Ignoring the pain in his side, he aimed his weapon at the man who had tormented Grace for so long. If Jason was up there it meant only one thing.

Suicide.

And Matthew knew there was no way Jason was ending his life and not taking Grace along with him.

"Jason Yamagada, it's the police," he yelled out.

The figure froze, and in the lights his friends shone on the man he could see that Jason was alone.

His insides turned to ice.

Where was Grace?

There was no way Jason would be up there without her if he intended to take his own life.

"You're too late," Jason called out. "It's already done. She's an angel now. She's mine."

"Where is she, Jason?" Matthew asked, surprised his voice was able to come out strong and confident when inside he was shattering into a million pieces.

"She's mine, detective, for all eternity. She always was, she was the only one who ever saw me." There was a peace to Jason's voice that he didn't like one bit. The man was too confident, and Matthew was terrified that he was right and that they were already too late to find Grace.

"You need to come down, Jason. We can talk about what happened, about what you did, get you help, but to do that you need to come down here," Matthew ordered.

"I'm sorry, detective, I can't do that. It's time. It's my time, I'm finally at peace."

With that, Jason held his arms out wide like wings and dived off the top of the house as though he were diving into a pool.

A second later the man's head slammed into the ground.

Matthew didn't bother going to check if Jason was alive, there was no way the man could have survived the headfirst fall. He would have broken his neck on impact in addition to the head trauma. Instead, he ran to the front door. It was locked, but a kick splintered the wooden door and he was inside.

"Grace?" he yelled. There was no way he could accept that she was gone, not until he was holding her lifeless body.

Elijah and Allina were behind him, yelling out her name as they cleared the downstairs and then moved up.

It was the second bedroom he went into when his heart began to stutter in his chest.

There was blood on the bed.

Clothes he remembered thrusting at Grace after he got the text that the safehouse was being shot at were tossed on the floor.

But there was no Grace.

"Where is she?" he demanded to no one in particular.

"She has to be here somewhere," Allina said, sounding like she was doing as terrible a job at clinging to control as he was.

"He killed her, he told us he did," Elijah said, soul shattering grief in his voice.

"Then where is she?" Matthew asked frantically, spinning in a slow circle as though she were going to materialize out of thin air.

"If Jason killed himself here then Grace is somewhere on the property," Allina said, making attempts to talk this through like they would any other case even though this wasn't just any case to any one of them.

"We checked the house and she's not in here," he reminded her.

"The yard?" Of all the ways Jason could have killed himself he'd chosen something outside, did that mean that Grace was out there as well?

He hurried to the window and scanned the backyard. There was a pool, and his first thought was that Jason had drowned her before going up on the roof, but then his gaze fell on an angel water feature surrounded by what looked like freshly planted rose bushes.

"He called her an angel," he said, already spinning around and flying through the house.

The others followed him out into the backyard and over to the area between two large trees along the back fence. The dirt beneath the rose bushes and angel water feature looked like it had been freshly worked over, was it possible that Jason had buried her there?

"She's here," he said with a certainty he felt down to his bones. There was a shovel leaning against one of the tree trunks and he grabbed it and started digging up the rose bushes.

"If he buried her, then she's already gone, Matthew," Elijah said, his voice heavy with grief.

"Maybe not," he said, tossing one rose bush aside and moving on to the second. There were three bushes planted on either side of the water feature, like Jason had made Grace's final resting place a memorial.

"Why else would he bury her?" Allina asked.

"He's had her for hours." The second rose bush came free, and he threw it aside. "If he killed her when he first took her then he would already have been dead by the time we got here." The third bush joined the others and he moved to the other side of the stone angel. "He chose this moment to end his own life. There's only one reason I can think of that he'd do that." Picking up the fourth rose bush, he barely noticed the thorns pricking his skin as he threw it away.

"You think he buried her alive? Then waited until he thought she'd be gone before killing himself?" Elijah asked.

"I think he wasn't ready to go until he and Grace could go together," he said as he dug up the fifth bush and moved on to the final one. "He wanted Grace to have a beautiful resting place, in his mind she was his angel." He gestured to the water feature as the last bush came free and he threw it to join the others. "Help me move this," he said grabbing hold of the water feature. "Burying someone alive isn't an exact science. He has no way of knowing exactly what moment she takes her final breath. You can live approximately five hours in a coffin after being buried alive. If he was preparing to jump when we got here, then it's been about five hours since he put her down here. There's still a chance she's alive."

Matthew prayed with everything he had that she was.

How unfair could the Universe be to have Grace take her last breath while they were driving down the street ready to rescue her?

Together he, Elijah, and Allina lifted the stone angel and moved it away. The second it was gone he started digging.

No way was he giving up on Grace.

No way.

There was a chance she was alive and that was what he was going to cling to.

The others joined him, he had no idea where they found shovels, nor did he care, his whole focus was on getting to Grace.

Please be alive, sweetheart.

They were down about four feet when the shovel hit something other than dirt.

"I think we got her," he announced.

Everyone picked up the speed, shoveling dirt out of the hole as fast as they could, with a desperation that you could feel in the air.

She had to be alive, she had to be. Her death would destroy not just him but her entire family. Grace's mix of strength and fragility was beautiful, and the bright light she shone into the world was something that would be noticeably missed. The world would be a worse place without her in it.

The coffin lid became exposed, Matthew lifted it, and saw Grace's still form lying inside. Her bruised and bloody hands rested between her bare breasts. What a horrific ordeal it would have been, trapped inside, knowing you were going to die, but having no way to stop it.

He didn't pause to check for a pulse, just scooped her up and took hold of the hand Elijah held out, no doubt to take his sister, but there was no way Matthew was letting go of the woman he loved.

Once he was out of the hole, he laid her down, pressing his fingers against her slender neck, while he held his cheek just above her mouth.

At first, he didn't feel anything.

Then it was there.

The faintest of pulses.

"She's got a pulse, but she's not breathing," he told the others as he shifted positions, so he was kneeling beside her head. It would be the cruelest of jokes to lose her now, when she must have taken her final breath while they were digging her out, unaware that help was mere moments away.

Matthew covered her mouth with his own, pinched her nose closed, and breathed into her, sharing his life with her, willing her to take a breath, to stay with him.

The first breath did nothing, so he covered her mouth again and breathed into her a second time.

"Come on, baby, don't leave me," he whispered as he smoothed a curl off her face. Her skin was still warm, and while her heart was still beating, if she didn't take a breath soon, he was going to lose her. Elijah knelt beside her and cut the ropes binding her wrists.

The second breath did nothing.

Again, he covered her mouth and forced air into her starving lungs.

Third time was the charm.

10:31 P.M.

Something warm forced its way inside her.

For some reason Grace wasn't afraid.

The terror of being buried alive had faded and she found herself hovering in a fluffy, white blanket.

Peace.

That's what it felt like.

Only it was a peace unlike anything she had ever experienced before.

This peace was all encompassing. It touched every part of her and wrapped her up all nice and snug. It took away every fear, every doubt, every regret and replaced them with a calm that seemed to inhabit her, possess her even.

Was she dead?

Was this Heaven?

Grace was almost afraid to open her eyes and take a look around her. The complete and utter darkness of the coffin was still fresh in her mind. The horror she'd felt in those long hours lying in there, unable to move, knowing with each breath she took she consumed a little more of the precious oxygen supply she had left, it felt detached. Like she had experienced those things and yet she hadn't.

But if she opened her eyes, she might find she was back in that dark place.

She couldn't stand that.

Not now that she'd had a taste of this peace.

The warmth rushed through her body again and this time it was accompanied by a faint buzzing sound.

Bees?

No, not bees.

A voice.

Only there were no voices in the coffin, only her own desperate screams for mercy, the echo of her weeping, and then the harsh rasp of each breath she took.

"Come on, baby, don't leave me."

The words resounded through her like a sledgehammer. There was so much pain in them, pain she felt even as she continued to remain cocooned in this warm, safe place.

Another rush of warmth filled her body only this time it was accompanied by a rush of strength.

Grace drew in a ragged breath, her eyes opened, and she found herself back in the darkness. Only this time it felt different. The peace was still there.

"Hey, baby, welcome back." Hands covered her cheeks, fingers caressing gently, infusing warmth with every stroke. Then there were lips, first they touched her forehead, and then they whispered across her lips in the gentlest of kisses.

There was no doubt in her mind who was holding her in their arms, who was touching her with such tender love, kissing her as though she were the oxygen they needed to live.

It was Matthew.

Somehow, he had found her, and somehow, she was still alive when he did, although she had a feeling it was only because of Matthew that she was currently sitting here in his lap, breathing.

"Matthew," she murmured, her voice was nothing but a soft rasp, and the word felt torn from her raw throat. She'd screamed so long and so hard when she first realized the hopelessness and horror of her situation that she'd made herself hoarse.

"Shh, baby, don't talk right now, just rest. Aww, baby, I almost lost you."

She felt him shift her, hold her closer, tighter, and there was no way she was complaining. This was exactly where she wanted to be.

It was where she had been so sure she would never get to be again.

"I was so scared," she whispered. Tears welled in her eyes, and she didn't bother holding them back. Maybe she had finally learned that there was no strength in holding in her emotions, strength just came from loving those around you and allowing them to love you in return. She could rebuild her life while still acknowledging the damage Jason had caused her.

"I know, honey, I know. I was terrified I was going to lose you." A shudder rocked through his body, she felt it because she was plastered against him.

"You saved me. I love you, Matthew." She looked up at him in the dark. Light from the moon streamed down around them as well as light from flashlights, she could see him well enough that she could see there were tear tracks on his cheeks.

She'd never seen him cry.

Reaching out, she touched the pad of her thumb to the wetness.

"You're crying," she said, almost incredulously.

"Yeah, babe, I'm crying. I love you, and I came seconds away from losing you."

"You love me?" She'd thought he did, was sure she felt it in his touches, and the way he looked at her, but she had needed to hear the words. She hadn't even realized how much until he said them.

"You doubted that?"

"No," she whispered. Her throat hurt, her hands ached, there was a burning pain in her back from the lashes of Jason's whip, but despite it all, the peace she'd felt while she was hovering between life and death was still there. For the first time in so many years she actually felt like everything was going to be okay. "I didn't doubt that."

Matthew smiled, palmed her cheek, and brushed a kiss across her lips. "Good, because you're going to need to get used to hearing it. I'm going to be saying it all the time."

"Good." She stared into Matthew's eyes, almost mesmerized by the love shining so brightly from them. She'd never been in love before, she'd never felt this kind of connection before, and it was a heady rush, making her almost giddy.

Someone cleared their throat, and for the first time she realized that she and Matthew weren't alone. Elijah and Ali were standing above them, looking down at her, tears on their cheeks as well.

Elijah held out a blanket and Grace realized she was naked. Maybe she should be embarrassed but to be honest she was too happy to be alive to really worry about anything else.

Her brother wrapped the blanket around her, tucking it in, then he hugged her hard. Grace hugged him back but appreciated that Elijah didn't try to take her out of Matthew's arms, showing his respect for her relationship with him, and in doing so giving his blessing. While she had never needed her brothers' blessing to do anything, the fact that they were supporting her relationship with Matthew meant the world to her. They'd always been like extra dads to her, and after their father's death they'd stepped up even more, and she hoped one day soon they might be walking her down the aisle.

Ali hugged her next, and again her sister-in-law didn't try to move her out of Matthew's arms. Just held onto her, whispered how much she loved her and then stood back, smiling down at her while Elijah wrapped his arms around his wife.

Grace snuggled into Matthew's arms, content just to rest her head on his shoulder, and allow him to take care of her.

For so long she'd had to be strong, take care of herself, there had been no one else there to do it for her. While she knew there would never be a time where she didn't feel guilt for the lives of the women Jason had forced her to kill, she knew that she hadn't had any choice. Jason was responsible for their deaths, not her, and she would tell herself as many times as she had to until it started to sink in.

Matthew would remind her too. She already knew he would be an amazing partner. He was compassionate, caring, and intuitive, he understood her better than she would have thought someone could in such a short time. He had his own demons to battle, but she knew that side by side, hand in hand, they were a powerful team, certainly strong enough to fight her demons and his.

Even with the shadows of their pasts hovering behind them, it didn't mean the future couldn't be bright and sunny. In fact, she was determined to make sure it was just that.

Sirens started to fill the air, and she felt Matthew shift, his muscles bunching, then he stood with her in his arms. It was only when she heard his muffled grunt of pain that she remembered he'd been shot.

"Are you okay? Put me down. Jason shot you, I was so scared you were dead," she babbled, trying to wriggle out of his arms. How could she have forgotten that Matthew had been hurt? She shouldn't have been lying all over him.

"I think you're fighting a losing battle, Gracie," Elijah said, amusement in his tone.

"Your brother's right, sweetheart, I'm not putting you down, not for anything. I'm alive, I'm okay, in a bit of pain, but there is nothing in this world that would make me let go of you right now. So put that pretty little head of yours back on my shoulder, close your eyes, and get some rest. You're the one who almost died, Grace, not me. So you're going to stay right here in my arms, I'm going to sit on the stretcher with you in the ambulance, and I might let go of you long enough for a doctor to examine you when we get to the hospital. I want to hold you, Grace, I need to, so stop fighting me."

She stopped.

What was the point?

Matthew needed to hold her, and she needed to be held.

Grace rested her head on his shoulder, and let Matthew carry her away from her would be grave.

CHAPTER
Ten

July 15th
11:12 A.M.

"I think you should have stayed in the hospital at least another day," Matthew said, casting a glance at Grace, who was sitting in the passenger seat of his car.

"You weren't staying," she reminded him.

"I wasn't the one who stopped breathing." For as long as he lived, he didn't think he would completely get over the image of Grace lying on the dirt while he knelt above her forcing air into her lungs and willing her to take a breath.

"No, you were just the one who got shot." There was the same stark fear in Grace's eyes that he knew was in his own. They'd almost lost one another before they even had a chance to let this thing between them grow into something amazing. "There was so much blood, I thought for sure I was going to lose you."

The pain in her soft voice tore at him. He wanted to make it better, take that pain from her, but he knew there was no way he could do that.

Just like there was no way she could take away from him the pain of knowing he'd been literally a minute away from losing her.

One minute.

That was all that it would have taken and his efforts to revive her might not have worked. Or if he had managed to get her breathing again, she might have sustained brain damage.

She was his miracle, and he was going to be grateful every day that she was still with him.

"I agree," Grace said.

"About what? I didn't say anything."

"I know that look on your face, you're thinking how lucky we both were, and how we should focus on being grateful rather than obsessing over what could have happened, and I agree. Neither of us are going to forget, both of us will have scars. There will be moments when we cry and rage over what Jason put us through, but you're right, we need to keep focusing on the good. We're alive and Jason is dead. He can't come after me again, and he can't hurt anyone who he feels is in his way. I'd say we are both pretty lucky."

"Amen." He reached out and Grace took his hand, lacing their fingers together. It felt like the most natural thing in the world to have her there beside him.

"My brothers didn't want me to come home with you," Grace said after they'd driven in silence for a few minutes.

After getting to the hospital last night, she'd been checked out and admitted. She'd insisted he sleep in the bed with her, and he hadn't been about to pass up that opportunity. They'd both crashed for a solid eight hours sleep, and this morning she'd announced that if he would have her she'd like to stay with him.

Of course, he'd wanted nothing more than to have her in his home. Heidi had ordered him to take a month off to recover from the gunshot wound, and what better way to spend that time than with Grace? Her brothers had tried to pitch the idea of her staying with them for a while longer, but he hadn't said anything, wanting it to be Grace's decision.

"They support us, but they're worried that someone is going to get hurt," Grace added.

"Of course they worry about you and things between us have

happened pretty quickly, much quicker than either of us were antic-ipating."

"I think they're more worried about you getting hurt then me."

"Really? Why?"

"Because they like you and they know you're a good guy. I think they're worried that my feelings aren't real, that it's just because you saved me and therefore you make me feel safe. That once I get my feet beneath me, I won't need you anymore." She tightened her grip on his hand, her voice began imploring. "I want you to know that it's not true. My feelings are real and they're not going anywhere. When I thought I was going to die, my last thoughts were of you, of everything we wouldn't get to do."

"I know your feelings are real, Grace," he assured her. While he didn't want her worrying that he doubted her, he had to admit it felt nice to know that her family cared about him enough to not want him to get hurt. It had been a long time since he had a family to care. "If you'd rather go home with them, I'll understand."

"No, I'm right where I want to be. I love my family so much, and I know they love me which is why I promised them I'd talk to them every day and see them as often as I could. Which reminds me that I have to see about getting my license back and getting a car."

There was so much Grace needed to do to rebuild her life, and he was so honored that she had chosen to have him by her side while she did that. "Tomorrow we'll go shopping, buy you whatever you need, clothes, toiletries, whatever you're going to need to make my home feel like our home, but today I just want to lock ourselves away from the rest of the world."

"Sounds perfect," Grace murmured and all of a sudden, the car was filled with a simmering sexual tension.

That tension ratcheted up several notches when Grace tugged her hand free from his and settled it in his lap, stroking him through his jeans. She was a little minx his sweet Grace, despite everything that had happened to her she was learning to be confident again, both in her desire to rebuild all she'd lost and in her sexuality.

"Grace," he warned as his body began to respond to her gentle touch.

"Yeah?" she asked, innocence personified. "You don't like?"

"Oh, you know I like, babe, but I'm driving, and you've been through a lot, you don't have to do this."

Her fingers moved to his zipper, and he sucked in a breath as her fingertips touched his bare skin. "Does it seem like I'm doing something I don't want to do?"

From the sexy purr of her voice to the way she touched him, it was abundantly clear that she was doing exactly what she wanted to be doing.

There was no way he wouldn't respond to her touch, and he quickly grew hard as her strokes grew firmer and faster. It was obvious that she was determined to make him come and he wanted to give her what she wanted.

"Word of warning, sweetheart, as soon as I get you alone, I'm going to enjoy my payback."

Her fingers trembled and her voice was breathy, "I look forward to it. I'm ready to make new memories, I'm ready to enjoy life, I'm not going to bury my head in the sand and pretend that what Jason did won't affect me for the rest of my life, but I want to be happy. I want to be free."

As she spoke her hand moved faster up and down his length, swirling the pad of her thumb over his tip. He felt pleasure building at the base of his spine. "I'm going to come, sweetheart," he warned.

"Good, I want to watch you fall apart, I want to bring you pleasure, I want to make good things happen," she whispered, and he knew the last was her way of trying to let go of her guilt over the lives she had been forced to take.

He wanted to give her power over her guilt, power to take the first step in releasing its hold on her, power to control her own life, giving what she wanted of her own free will and not because she was forced to.

Letting go, Matthew allowed himself to take the pleasure Grace was offering knowing that he was helping her in the process.

The orgasm hit hard and fast, momentarily stealing his breath and it was everything he could do to keep control of the car and not send them crashing into another car, or a pedestrian, or whatever else got in their way.

When he was able to think of anything other than keeping the car on the road, he glanced over at Grace to find her smiling smugly as she removed her hand from inside his pants. Given the bruising and broken nails from her fighting against the coffin lid, she really shouldn't have done that, but it was clear it meant a lot to her.

"Come here," he said, reaching for her hand.

"You're supposed to be driving."

"You weren't worrying about that a second ago. I warned you honey." Keeping one hand on the steering wheel his other slipped up under her dress. "You're not wearing panties," he groaned.

Grace laughed. "I tried but the band kept pressing against the wounds on my back, it was uncomfortable, so I didn't bother. Besides, we were only going back to your place, I didn't think I needed them."

"You didn't. In fact, you should never wear panties again, so I always have easy access to this." He traced her entrance, found it already wet and ready for him and slipped a finger inside.

A sexy little moan fell from her lips and as he slid his finger deeper and pressed his thumb against her little bundle of nerves she sucked her bottom lip between her teeth, chewing on it in the most adorable way.

Matthew added a second finger, stretched her, teased her, increasing the pressure on her hard little bud.

Her breathing became choppy, her fingers curled into fists, and he could feel her internal muscles trembling.

"Come for me, baby," he said as he curled his fingers around so he could find that spot inside her he knew would be guaranteed to make her fall apart.

Which she did.

He didn't let up, working her as she rode out the wave of ecstasy until she finally sagged in her seat, only then did he remove his hand, sticking his fingers in her mouth and sucking, enjoying the flare of heat in Grace's blue eyes.

"Did we really just make out while you're driving the car?" she asked with a lazy smile.

"Yeah, we did."

"I liked it. I liked being wild, being free. I like being with you."

He reached out and took her hand again. "You know the best part, sweetheart? We have a whole lifetime ahead of us to be wild and free. An entire lifetime." Which sounded pretty perfect as far as he was concerned.

~

12:00 P.M.

Grace felt something growing inside her that hadn't been there before.

A strength, a determination, maybe one that came from knowing she hadn't given up, she hadn't shied away from playing bait, and while it hadn't worked out the way any of them had hoped in the end Jason had been taken care of and she was now free. A week ago, she had been determined to rebuild her life, but now she could admit she was running from her feelings, pretending she wasn't as affected by her ordeal as she was.

No more running.

Now she was ready to face what had happened to her while, at the same time, still rebuild the life that had been stolen from her and reclaiming control.

"I was thinking that maybe I'd see about joining a support group for survivors," she told Matthew. "It's hard to talk to someone who can't really understand what I went through, so I thought that was better than trying another counselor. I'm not counting it out, and maybe I'll even get a good recommendation from another survivor, but I don't want to pretend that I'm fine anymore. I'm not fine, but I also know I will be. I have the best family ever, and I have you. I have everything I need to rebuild my life, and if it's a struggle to get there, then I know I'll grow stronger as I walk that path."

"I'm so proud of you, do you know that? You're amazing, an inspiration, and you're going to be a great therapist. You're going to save lives, do you realize that? Not just other survivors like you but the lives of everyone who loves them too. I'm so in awe of you, you're completely amazing. I want you to know that it's never a weakness to struggle or to ask for help. You have so many people who are there for you, who will drop everything to give you what you need, so I want you to promise me something."

"Anything."

"There are going to be dark days over the coming weeks and months, probably for both of us, but I want you to promise me that on those dark days, where the burden seems too heavy to carry for another second and you just want to give up, on those days I want you to reach out to me, tell me, let me help you hold that burden."

"Promise," Grace said without hesitation. "You promise me the same. Your mom and sister messed up when they weren't grateful to you for saving their lives, that's their loss. But you're not alone anymore, Matthew. You have me and you have my whole family. So, when you're feeling unlovable and you want to shut everyone out, I want you to reach out to me, tell me, let *me* help *you* hold that burden."

"Promise."

"I love you."

"I love you more, honey."

"I don't think that's possible." It was the craziest thing, when she had first woken in the hospital she'd felt so broken inside, disconnected, damaged, like she would never be able to be a normal person. Then Matthew had started coming around, being sweet, making her laugh, treating her like she was just another person instead of a victim, sharing his deepest secrets with her, and all of a sudden, she was falling in love with him.

"Here we go, home sweet home," Matthew announced as he turned into the driveway of a two-story house. It was painted a bright crisp white, the garden was simple, just a neatly mowed lawn, but there was a cute arbor covered in a flowered vine at the garden gate giving it a warm and inviting feel. She could already see herself being happy living here. Matthew was off work for a month, and while they both had injuries to recover from, maybe they could spend some of their time doing a little gardening, planting those flower beds she'd been thinking about. If Matthew was happy for her to start putting her stamp on their home that was.

Ali and Laynie had packed up her clothes from Jem and Laynie's house and brought them by the hospital, so as they got out of the car,

Matthew went to the back and grabbed her suitcase, then he took her hand and together they headed for the house. It had a huge front porch that ran the width of the building. On one side of the front door was a small table and two chairs, on the other was a large porch swing she could already tell was going to become one of her favorite places to curl up on a warm summer's evening.

"Oh, I almost forgot," Matthew said, setting down her bags and scooping her up into his arms. "I know we're not newlyweds, but this is still the beginning of our lives together and I want to do it right."

One handed, he unlocked the door, his lips finding hers as he pushed it open. Grace was already feeling her body growing hot and needy, a throbbing started between her legs, and she was about to suggest they head straight upstairs to the bedroom, when ...

"Welcome home!"

The cacophony of voices drew her attention and she turned to find the foyer filled with her family and their friends. Friends that might one day be her friends. Elijah and Jeremiah were there, of course, along with Ali and Laynie. Then there were some people she'd met and others who she'd only heard of and seen pictures of from her family. There was Ali's partner Jonathon, his wife Clara, and their seventeen-month-old son Kyle. There was Clara's sister Naomi and her husband Sam, and their six-month-old daughter Daveli, and Clara and Naomi's other sister Aggie and her husband Nick and their two-month-old son Ryan. There was Nick's brother Luke, and his heavily pregnant wife Summer, and Matthew's partner Rylla, her husband Nate, Rylla's thirteen-year-old niece and ten-year-old nephew who the couple was raising. Rylla's hand rested almost absently on her stomach and Matthew had told her that his partner had just found out she was expecting.

So many smiling faces, and while she didn't know most of them, they had still showed up today to support her. They'd put their lives on the line to try to keep her safe, they were people she wanted to get to know, who she hoped would become friends, part of her and Matthew's extended family.

"Please tell me you didn't marry my sister," Elijah teased, and it was nice to see him relaxed, like the brother she remembered and not the stressed-out man who had worried over her the last several days.

"Not yet," Matthew said with a grin as he set her on her feet.

Before she could tell him to name the time and place and she'd be there, the pitter-patter of paws sounded and a large German Shepherd with the softest looking fur and the cutest pair of ears made its way through the crowd of people.

A dog?

Her eyes flew to Laynie's, who was holding the leash. Her sister-in-law had mentioned the possibility of looking into getting her a protection dog, but with everything that had happened the last couple of days she'd completely forgotten. Could this ...?

"Her name is Leila and she's two years old. She's trained as a protection dog. You'll have to do some training with her so you learn all of her commands and how to practice them so she doesn't get rusty, but she's all yours," Laynie informed her, handing over the leash.

"Mine?" Grace held the leash but didn't allow herself to touch the dog yet. Yes, she'd told her siblings she wanted a dog, but it wasn't something she and Matthew had talked about, and he might not want a dog living in his house. She'd planned on getting her own place and she didn't even know if Matthew liked dogs. She looked up at him. "If you don't ..."

He touched a finger to her lips. "I knew about the dog. I've always wanted a pet but I just never had the time to put into one. Between the two of us we should be able to make it work between my job, yours, and your studies. Besides, I'll feel better on nights when I'm not here to know you're not alone, that you have a protection dog by your side."

Grace threw her arms around him and kissed him hard on the lips, rolling her eyes at the oohs and ahhs sounding behind them. Then she dropped to her knees beside the dog and held out her hand. Leila sniffed it curiously and then rested her head on Grace's shoulder and she wrapped her arms around the dog's neck, already in love with the sweet natured girl.

This was perfect.

After years of crippling loneliness, trapped in a nightmare she had been sure she was never going to escape. Now she had a dog in her arms who she already knew was going to become her best friend and confidant, she was surrounded by people, both family and not, who cared about her, and she had a man standing behind her, his hand gently stroking her curls, who already lived inside her heart.

She had a feeling she would never be alone again.

Want more hot cops, tough heroines, serial killers, suspense and mystery?
Check out my Christmas Romantic Suspense series, romantic suspense Christmas style!

Christmas Hostage (Christmas Romantic Suspense #1)

Also by Jane Blythe

Detective Parker Bell Series

A SECRET TO THE GRAVE

WINTER WONDERLAND

DEAD OR ALIVE

LITTLE GIRL LOST

FORGOTTEN

Count to Ten Series

ONE

TWO

THREE

FOUR

FIVE

SIX

BURNING SECRETS

SEVEN

EIGHT

NINE

TEN

Broken Gems Series

CRACKED SAPPHIRE

CRUSHED RUBY

FRACTURED DIAMOND

SHATTERED AMETHYST

SPLINTERED EMERALD

SALVAGING MARIGOLD

River's End Rescues Series

COCKY SAVIOR

SOME REGRETS ARE FOREVER

SOME FEARS CAN CONTROL YOU

SOME LIES WILL HAUNT YOU

SOME QUESTIONS HAVE NO ANSWERS

SOME TRUTH CAN BE DISTORTED

SOME TRUST CAN BE REBUILT

SOME MISTAKES ARE UNFORGIVABLE

Candella Sisters' Heroes Series

LITTLE DOLLS

LITTLE HEARTS

LITTLE BALLERINA

Storybook Murders Series

NURSERY RHYME KILLER

FAIRYTALE KILLER

FABLE KILLER

Saving SEALs Series

SAVING RYDER

SAVING ERIC

SAVING OWEN

SAVING LOGAN

SAVING GRAYSON

SAVING CHARLIE

Prey Security Series

PROTECTING EAGLE

PROTECTING RAVEN

PROTECTING FALCON

PROTECTING SPARROW

PROTECTING HAWK

PROTECTING DOVE

Prey Security: Alpha Team Series

DEADLY RISK

LETHAL RISK

EXTREME RISK

FATAL RISK

COVERT RISK

SAVAGE RISK

Prey Security: Artemis Team Series

IVORY'S FIGHT

PEARL'S FIGHT

LACEY'S FIGHT

OPAL'S FIGHT

Prey Security: Bravo Team Series

VICIOUS SCARS

RUTHLESS SCARS

Christmas Romantic Suspense Series

CHRISTMAS HOSTAGE

CHRISTMAS CAPTIVE

CHRISTMAS VICTIM

YULETIDE PROTECTOR

YULETIDE GUARD

YULETIDE HERO

HOLIDAY GRIEF

Conquering Fear Series (Co-written with Amanda Siegrist)

DROWNING IN YOU

OUT OF THE DARKNESS

CLOSING IN

About the Author

USA Today bestselling author Jane Blythe writes action-packed romantic suspense and military romance featuring protective heroes and heroines who are survivors. One of Jane's most popular series includes Prey Security, part of Susan Stoker's OPERATION ALPHA world! Writing in that world alongside authors such as Janie Crouch and Riley Edwards has been a blast, and she looks forward to bringing more books to this genre, both within and outside of Stoker's world. When Jane isn't binge-reading she's counting down to Christmas and adding to her 200+ teddy bear collection!

To connect and keep up to date please visit any of the following

www.ingramcontent.com/pod-product-compliance
Lightning Source LLC
Chambersburg PA
CBHW032003240626
47153CB00003B/1103